Jack Higg…
Leaving sc…
the Royal …
man borde… war. His subsequent employment included occupations as diverse as circus roustabout, truck driver, clerk and, after taking an honours degree in sociology and social psychology, teacher and university lecturer.

The Eagle Has Landed turned him into an international bestselling author, and his novels have since sold over 250 million copies and have been translated into fifty-five languages. Many of them have also been made into successful films. His recent bestselling novels include *Pay the Devil, Day of Reckoning, Edge of Danger, Midnight Runner, The Keys of Hell* and *Bad Company.*

In 1995 Jack Higgins was awarded an honorary doctorate by Leeds Metropolitan University. He is a fellow of the Royal Society of Arts and an expert scuba diver and marksman. He lives on Jersey.

Also by Jack Higgins

The Valhalla Exchange
To Catch a King
Dillinger
The Run to Morning
The Eagle Has Landed
A Prayer for the Dying
The Last Place God Made
Storm Warning
Day of Judgement
Solo
Luciano's Luck
Touch the Devil
Exocet
Confessional
Night of the Fox
A Season in Hell
Memoirs of a Dance-Hall Romeo
Cold Harbour
The Eagle Has Flown
Eye of the Storm
Thunder Point
On Dangerous Ground
Sheba
Angel of Death
Drink with the Devil
Year of the Tiger
The President's Daughter
Flight of Eagles
The White House Connection
Pay the Devil
Day of Reckoning
Edge of Danger
The Keys of Hell
Midnight Runner
Bad Company
A Fine Night for Dying

JACK HIGGINS

TOLL FOR THE BRAVE

HarperCollins*Publishers*

This novel is entirely a work of fiction.
The names, characters and incidents portrayed in it are the work of the author's imagination. Any resemblance to actual persons, living or dead, events or localities is entirely coincidental.

HarperCollins*Publishers*
77–85 Fulham Palace Road,
Hammersmith, London W6 8JB

www.harpercollins.co.uk

This paperback edition 2004
5

First published under the name Harry Patterson
by John Long 1971

First published in paperback by Arrow 1977

Set in Sabon by Palimpsest Book Production Limited,
Polmont, Stirlingshire

Printed and bound in Great Britain by
Clays Ltd, St Ives plc

Publisher's Note

TOLL FOR THE BRAVE was first published in the UK by John Long, London, in 1971 under the authorship of Harry Patterson. The author was, in fact, the writer familiar to modern readers as Jack Higgins. Harry Patterson was one of the names he used during his early writing days. The book was later published in paperback by Arrow – under the authorship of Jack Higgins – but it has been out of print for several years.

In 2004, it seemed to the author and his publishers that it was a pity to leave such a good story languishing on his shelves. So we are delighted to be able to bring back TOLL FOR THE BRAVE for the pleasure of the vast majority of us who never had a chance to read the earlier editions.

Nightmare

Prologue

They were beating the Korean to death in the next room, all attempts to break him down having failed completely. He was a stubborn man and, like most of his countrymen, held the Chinese in a kind of contempt and they reacted accordingly. The fact that Republic of Korea troops had the highest kill ratio in Vietnam at that time didn't exactly help matters.

There were footsteps outside, the door opened and a young Chinese officer appeared. He snapped his fingers and I got up like a good dog and went to heel. A couple of guards were dragging the Korean away by the feet, a blanket wrapped about his head to keep the blood off the floor. The officer paused to light a cigarette, ignoring me completely, then walked along the corridor and I shuffled after him.

We passed the interrogation room, which was something to be thankful for, and stopped outside the camp commandant's office at the far end. The young officer knocked, pushed me inside and closed the door.

Colonel Chen-Kuen was writing away busily at his desk. He ignored me for quite some time, then put down his pen and got to his feet. He walked to the window and glanced outside.

'The rains are late this year.'

I couldn't think of anything to say in answer to that pearl of wisdom, didn't even know if it was expected. In any event, he didn't give me a chance to make small talk and carried straight on, still keeping his back to me.

'I am afraid I have some bad news for you, Ellis. I have finally received instructions from Central Committee in Hanoi. Both you and General St Claire are to be executed this morning.'

He turned, his face grave, concerned and said a whole lot more, though whether or not he was expressing his personal regret, I could not be sure for it was as if I had cut the wires, his mouth opening and closing soundlessly and I didn't hear a word.

He left me. In fact, it was the last time I ever saw him. When the door opened next I thought it might be the guards come to take me, but it wasn't. It was Madame Ny.

She was wearing a uniform that looked anything but People's Republic and had obviously been tailored by someone who knew his business. Leather boots, khaki shirt and a tunic which had been cut to show off those good breasts of hers to the best advantage. The dark eyes were wet with tears, tragic in the white face.

She said, 'I'm sorry, Ellis.'

Funny, but I almost believed her. Almost, but not quite. I moved in close so that I wouldn't miss, spat right in her face, opened the door and went out.

The young officer had disappeared, but a couple of guards were waiting for me. They were hardly more than boys, stocky little peasants out of the rice fields who gripped their AK assault rifles too tightly like men who weren't as used to them as they should be. One of them went ahead, opened the end door and motioned me through.

The compound was deserted, not a prisoner in sight. The gate stood wide, the watch towers floated in the morning mist. Everything waited. And then I heard the sound of marching feet and St Claire came round the corner with the young Chinese officer and two guards.

In spite of the broken jump boots, the tattered green fatigues, he still looked everything a soldier ever could be. He marched with that crisp, purposeful movement that only the regular seems to acquire. Every step meant something. It was as if the Chinese were with him; as if he were leading.

He had the Indian sign on them, there was no doubt of that, which is saying something for the Chinese do not care for the Negro overmuch. But then, he was something special and like no man I have known before or since.

He paused and looked at me searchingly, then smiled that famous St Claire smile that made you feel you were the only damned person that mattered in the wide world. I moved to his side and we set off together. He increased his pace and I had to jump to it to stay level with him. We might have been back at Benning, drill on the square, and the guards had to run to keep up with us.

Colonel Chen-Kuen's rains came as we went through the gate, in that incredible instant downpour that you only get with the monsoon. It didn't make the slightest difference to St Claire and he carried on at the same brisk pace so that one of the guards had to run past to get in front of us to lead the way.

In other circumstances it could have been funny, but not now. We plunged through the heavy, drenching downpour into the forest and took a path that led down towards the river a mile or more away.

A couple of hundred yards further on we entered a broad clearing that sloped steeply into the trees. There were mounds of earth all over the place, as nice a little cemetery as you could wish for, but minus the headstones naturally.

The young officer called us to a halt, his voice hard and flat through the rain. We stood and waited while he had a look round. There didn't seem much room to spare, but he obviously wasn't going to let a little thing like that worry him. He selected a spot on the far side of the clearing, found us a couple of rusting trenching shovels that looked as if they had seen plenty of service and went and stood in the shelter of the trees with two of the guards and smoked cigarettes, leaving one to watch over us as we set to work.

The soil was pure loam, light and easy to handle because of the rain. It lifted in great spadefuls that had me knee-deep in my own grave before I knew where I was. And St Claire wasn't exactly helping. He worked at it as if there was a bonus at the end of the job, those great arms of his swinging three spadefuls of dirt into the air for every one of mine.

The rain seemed to increase in a sudden rush that drowned all hope. I was going to die. The thought rose in my throat like bile to choke on and then it happened. The side of the trench next to me collapsed suddenly, probably because of the heavy rain, leaving a hand and part of a forearm protruding from the earth, flesh rotting from the bones.

I turned away blindly, fighting for air, and

lost my balance, falling flat on my face. At the same moment the other wall of the trench collapsed across me.

As I struggled for life, I was aware that St Claire had started to laugh, that deep, rich, special sound that seemed to come right up from the roots of his being. It didn't make any kind of sense at all but I had other things to think of now. The stink of the grave was in my nostrils, my eyes. I opened my mouth to scream and soil poured in choking the life out of me in a great wave of darkness that blotted out all light . . .

World's end

1

The dream always ended in exactly the same way – with me sitting bolt upright in bed, screaming like any child frightened in the dark, St Claire's laughter ringing in my ears which was the most disturbing thing of all.

And as always during the silence that followed, I waited with a kind of terrible anxiety for something to happen, something I dreaded above all things and yet could not put a name to.

But as usual, there was nothing. Only the rain brushing against the windows of the old house, driven by a wind that blew stiffly across the marshes from the North Sea. I listened, head turned, waiting for a sign that never came, shaking slightly and sweating rather a lot which was exactly how Sheila found me when she arrived a moment later.

She had been painting – still clutched a palette and three brushes in her left hand and the old terry towelling robe she habitually wore was streaked with paint. She put the palette and brushes down on a chair, came and sat on the edge of the bed, taking my hands in hers.

'What is it, love? The dream again?'

When I spoke my voice was hoarse and broken. 'Always the same – always. Accurate in every detail, exactly as it was until St Claire starts to laugh.'

I started to shake uncontrollably, teeth grinding together in intense stress. She had the robe off in a moment, was under the sheets, her arms pulling me into the warmth of that magnificent body.

And as always, she knew exactly what she was doing for fear turns upon itself endlessly like a mad dog unless the cycle can be broken. She kissed me repeatedly, hands gentle. For a little while, comfort, then by some mysterious alchemy, she was on her back, thighs spreading to receive me. An old story between us, but one which never palled and at such moments, the finest therapy in the world – or so I told myself.

Englishmen who have served with the American forces in Vietnam aren't exactly thick on the ground, but there are more of us around than most people realise. Having said that, to disclose what I'd been doing for the past three years, in mixed company, was usually calculated to raise most eyebrows, and in some instances could be guaranteed to provoke open hostility.

The party where I had first met Sheila Ward was a case in point. It had turned out to be a stuffy, pseudo-intellectual affair. I was thoroughly bored and didn't seem to know a soul except my hostess. When she finally had time for me I had done what seemed the sensible thing and got good and drunk, something at which I was fairly expert in those days.

Unfortunately, she didn't seem to notice and insisted on introducing me to a sociologist from the London School of Economics who by some minor miracle known only to academics, had managed to obtain a doctorate for a thesis on structural values in Revolutionary China without ever having actually visited the country.

The information that I had spent three of the best years of my young life serving with the American Airborne in Vietnam including a sizeable stretch in a North Vietnamese prison camp, had the same effect as if he had been hit by a rather heavy truck.

He told me that I was about as acceptable in his eyes as a lump of dung on his shoe which seemed to go down well with the group who'd been hanging on his every word, but didn't impress me one little bit.

I told him what he could do about it in pretty fluent Cantonese which – surprisingly in an expert on Chinese affairs – he didn't seem to understand.

But someone else did which was when I met Sheila Ward. Just about the most spectacular woman I'd ever seen in my life. Every man's fantasy dream. Soft black leather boots that reached to her thighs, a yard or two of orange wool posing as a dress, shoulder-length auburn hair framing a strong peasant face and a mouth which was at least half a mile wide. She could have been ugly, but her mouth was her saving grace. With that mouth she was herself alone.

'You can't do that to him,' she said in fair Chinese. 'They'd give you at least five years.'

'Not bad,' I told her gravely, 'but your accent is terrible.'

'Yorkshire,' she said. 'Just a working class girl from Doncaster on the make. My husband was a lecturer at Hong Kong University for five years.'

The conversation was interrupted by my sociologist friend who tried to pull her out of the way and started again so I punched him none too gently under the breastbone, knuckles extended, and he went down with a shrill cry.

I don't really remember what happened after that except that Sheila led me out and no one tried to get in the way. I do know that it was raining hard, that I was leaning up against my car in the alley at the side of the house beneath a street lamp.

She buttoned me into my trenchcoat and said soberly, 'You were pretty nasty in there.'

'A bad habit of mine these days.'

'You get in fights often?'

'Now and then.' I struggled to light a cigarette. 'I irritate people or they annoy me.'

'And afterwards you feel better?' She shook her head 'There are other ways of relieving that kind of tension or didn't it ever occur to you?'

She had a bright red oilskin mac slung around her shoulders against the rain so I reached inside and cupped a beautifully firm breast.

She said calmly, 'See what I mean?'

I leaned back against the car, my face up to the rain. 'I can do several things quite well besides belt people. Latin declensions which comes of having gone to the right kind of school and I can find true north by pointing the hour hand of my watch at the sun or by shoving a stick into the ground. And I can cook. My monkey is delicious and tree rats are my speciality.'

'Exactly my type,' she said. 'I can see we're going to get along fine.'

'Just one snag,' I told her. 'Bed.'

She frowned. 'You didn't lose anything when you were out there did you?'

'Everything intact and in full working order, ma'am.' I saluted gravely. 'It's just that I've never been any good at it. A Chinese psychiatrist once told me it was because my grandfather found me in bed with the Finnish au pair when I was fourteen and beat all hell out of me with a blackthorne he prized rather highly. Carried it all the way through the desert campaign. He was a general, you see, so he naturally found it difficult to forgive me when it broke.'

'On you?' she said.

'Exactly, so I don't think you'd find me very satisfactory.'

'We'll have to see, won't we?' She was suddenly the lass from Doncaster again, the Yorkshire voice flat in the rain. 'What do you do with yourself – for a living, I mean?'

'Is that what you call it?' I shrugged. 'The last of the dinosaurs. Hunted to extinction. I enjoy what used to be known in society as private means – lots of them. In what little time I have to spare, I also try to write.'

She smiled at that, looking so astonishingly beautiful that things actually stopped moving for a moment. 'You're just what I've been seeking for my old age.'

'You're marvellous,' I said. 'Also big, busty, sensuous . . .'

'Oh, definitely that,' she said. 'I never know when to stop. I'm also a lay-out artist in an advertising agency, divorced and thirty-seven years of age. You've only seen me in an artificial light, love.'

I started to slide down the side of the car and she got a shoulder under my arm and went through my clothes.

'You'll find the wallet in my left breast pocket,' I murmured.

She chuckled. 'You daft ha'p'orth. I'm looking for the car keys. Where do you live?'

'The Essex coast,' I told her. 'Foulness.'

'Good God,' she said. 'That must be all of fifty miles away.'

'Fifty-eight.'

She took me back to her flat in the King's Road, just for the night. I stayed a month, which was definitely all I could take of the hub of the universe, the bright lights, the crowds. I needed solitude again, the birds, the marshes, my own little hole to rot in. So she left her job at the agency, moved down to Foulness and set up house with me.

Oscar Wilde once said that life is a bad quarter of an hour made up of exquisite moments. She certainly gave me plenty of those in the months that followed and that morning was no exception. I started off in my usual frenzy and within minutes she had gentled me into making slow, meaningful love and with considerably more expertise than when we had first met. She'd definitely taken care of that department.

Afterwards I felt fine, the fears of the hour before dawn a vague fantasy already forgotten. I kissed her softly under her rigid left nipple, tossed the sheets to one side and went into the bathroom.

A medical friend once assured me that the shock of an ice-cold shower was detrimental to the vascular system and liable to reduce life expectancy by a month. Admittedly he was in his cups at the time but I had always found it an excellent excuse for spending five minutes each morning under a shower that was as hot as I could bear.

When I returned to the bedroom Sheila had gone, but I could smell coffee and realised that I was hungry. I dressed quickly and went into the sitting-room. There was a log fire burning on the stone hearth and she had her easel set up in front of it.

She was standing there now in her old terry towelling robe, the palette back in her left hand, dabbing vigorously at the canvas with a long brush.

'I'm having coffee,' she said without turning round. 'I've made tea for you. It's on the table.'

I poured myself a cup and went and stood behind her. It was good – damn good. A view from the house, the saltings splashed with sea-lavender, the peculiarly luminous light reflected by the slimy mud flats, blurring everything at the edges. Above all, the loneliness.

'It's good.'

'Not yet.' She worked away busily in one corner without turning her head. 'But it will be. What do you want for breakfast?'

'I wouldn't dream of disturbing the muse.' I

kissed her on the nape of the neck. 'I'll take Fritz for a walk.'

'All right, love.'

The brush was moving very quickly now, a frown of concentration on her face. I had ceased to exist so I got my hunting jacket from behind the door and left her to it.

I have been told that in some parts of America, Airedales are kept specifically to hunt bears and they are excellent swimmers, a useful skill in an area like Foulness. But not Fritz who was Sheila's one true love, a great, shaggy bundle in ginger and black, amiable to a degree in spite of a bark that could be heard half a mile away. He had ceased to frighten even the birds and was terrified of water, objecting to even the mildest wetting of his paws. He romped ahead of me along the rutted grassy track and I followed.

Foulness – Cape of Birds, the Saxons called it and they were here in plenty. I have always had a liking for solitude and no more than fifty-odd miles from London, I rotted gently and in the right place for it. Islands and mist and sea walls to keep out the tide, built by the Dutch centuries ago. Creeks, long grass, stirring to change colour as if brushed by an invisible presence, the gurgle of water everywhere and the sea creeping in like a ghost in the night to take the unwary.

The Romans had known this place, Saxon outlaws hidden here from the Normans, and now Ellis Jackson pretended for the moment that this was all there was.

In the marshes autumn is the saltings purple and mauve with the sea-lavender, the damp smell of rotting vegetation. Birds calling constantly, lifting from beyond the sea wall uneasily, summer dead and winter yet to come. Gales blowing in off the North Sea, the wind moaning endlessly.

Was this all there was – truly? A bottle a day and Sheila Ward to warm the bed? What was I waiting for, here at the world's end?

Somewhere in the far distance I heard shooting. Heavy stuff from the sound of it. It stirred something deep inside, set the adrenalin surging only I didn't have an MI6 carbine to hang on to and this wasn't the Mekong Delta. This was a grazing marsh on the tip of Foulness in quiet Essex and the shooting came from the Ministry of Defence Proof and Experimental Artillery ranges at Shoeburyness.

Fritz was somewhere up ahead exploring and out of sight. He suddenly appeared over a dyke about fifty yards ahead, plunged into a wide stretch of water and swam strongly to the other side, disappearing into the reeds.

A moment later, he started to bark frantically, a strange new sound for him that seemed to have fear in it. There was a single rifle shot and the barking ceased.

Birds lifted out of the marsh in great clouds. The beating of their wings filled the air and when they had passed, they left an uncanny stillness.

I ran into the mist calling his name. I found his body a minute later sprawled across the rutted track. From the look of things he had been shot through the head with a high velocity bullet for most of the skull had disintegrated. I couldn't really take it in because it didn't make any kind of sense. This wasn't a place where one found strangers. The Ministry were tough about that because of the experimental ranges. Even the locals had to produce a pass at certain checkpoints when leaving or returning to the general area. I had one myself.

A small wind touched my cheek coldly, there was a splashing and as I turned something moved in the tall reeds to my right.

North Vietnamese regular troops wear khaki, but the Viet Cong have their own distinctive garb of conical straw hat and black pyjamas. Many of them still use the old Browning Automatic rifle or the MI carbine that got most American troops through the Second World War.

But not the one who stepped out of the reeds some ten or fifteen yards to my right. He held what looked like a brand new AK47 assault rifle across his chest, the best that China could provide. Very probably the finest assault rifle in the world.

He was as small as they usually were, a stocky little peasant out of some rice field or other. He was soaked to the knees, rain dripped from the brim of his straw hat, the black jacket was quilted against the cold.

I took a couple of cautious steps back. He said

nothing, made no move at all, just stood there, holding the AK at the high port. I half-turned and found his twin standing ten yards to my rear.

If this was madness, it had been a long time coming. I cracked completely, gave a cry of fear, jumped from the track into the reeds and plunged into the mist, knee-deep in water.

A wild swan lifted in alarm, great wings beating so close to me that I cried out again and got my arms to my face. But I kept on moving, coming up out of the reeds on the far side close to the old grass-covered dyke that kept the sea back in its own place.

I crouched against it, listening for the sounds of pursuit. Somewhere back there in the marsh there was a disturbance, birds rising in alarm. It was enough. I scrambled over the dyke, dropped to the beach below and ran for my life.

Sheila was still at the easel in front of the fire when I burst into the cottage. I made it to a wing-backed chair near the door and fell into it. She was on her knees beside me in an instant.

'Ellis? Ellis, what is it?'

I tried to speak, but the words wouldn't come and there was real fear in her eyes now. She hurried to the sideboard and returned with a glass of whisky.

I spilled more than I got down, my hand shaking as if I was in high fever. I had left the door open behind me and it swung to and fro in the wind. As she got up to close it, there was the patter of feet.

She said, 'There's a lovely old boy and mud up to the eyebrows.'

Fritz padded round to the front of the chair and shoved his nose at my hand.

There had always been a chance that this would happen ever since Tay Son. The psychiatrists had hinted as much, for the damage was too deep. I started to cry helplessly like a child as Fritz nuzzled my hand.

Sheila was very pale now. She pushed my hair back from my brow as if I were a small untidy boy and kissed me gently.

'It's going to be all right, Ellis. Just trust me.'

The telephone was in the kitchen. I sat there, clutching my empty whisky glass, staring into space, tears running down my face.

I heard her say, 'American Embassy? I'd like to speak to General St Claire, please. My name is Mrs Sheila Ward. There was a pause and then she said, 'Max, is that you?' and closed the door.

She came out in two or three minutes and knelt in front of me. 'Max is coming, Ellis. He's leaving at once. He'll be here in an hour and a half at the most.'

She left me then to go and get dressed and I hung on to that thought. That Max was coming. Black Max. Brigadier-General James Maxwell St Claire, Congressional Medal of Honour, D.S.C., Silver Star, Medaille Militaire, from Anzio to Vietnam, every boy's fantasy figure. Black Max was coming to save me as he had saved me, body and soul, once before in the place they called Tay Son.

Forcing House Number One

2

On a wet February evening in 1966 during my second year at Sandhurst, I jumped from a railway bridge to a freight train passing through darkness below. I landed on a pile of coke, but the cadet who followed me wasn't so lucky. He dropped between two trucks and was killed instantly.

We were drunk, of course, which didn't help matters. It was the final link in a chain of similar stupidities and the end of something as far as I was concerned. Harsh words were said at the inquest, even harsher by the commandant when dismissing me from the Academy.

Words didn't exactly fail my grandfather either, who being a major-general, took it particularly hard. He had always considered me some kind of moral degenerate after the famous episode with the Finnish au pair at the tender age of fourteen and this final exploit gave him the pleasure of knowing that he had been right all along.

My father had died what is known as a hero's death at Arnhem during the Second World War. My mother, two years later. So, the old man had had his hands on me for some considerable time. Why he had always disliked me so was past knowing and yet hatred is as strong a bond as loving so that when he forbade me his house, there was a kind of release.

The army had been his idea, not mine. The family tradition, or the family curse depending which way you looked at it, so now I was free after twenty-odd years of some kind of servitude or other and thanks to my mother's money, wealthy by any standards.

Perhaps because of that – because it was my choice and mine alone – I flew to New York within a week of leaving the Academy and enlisted for a period of three years in the United States Army as a paratrooper.

* * *

It could be argued that the jump from that railway bridge was a jump into hell for in a sense it landed me in Tay Son, although eighteen months of a different kind of hell intervened.

I flew into the old French airport at Ton Son Nhut in July, 1966, one of two hundred replacements for the 801st Airborne Division. The pride of the army and every man a volunteer as paratroopers are the world over.

A year later, only forty-eight of that original two hundred were still on active duty. The rest were either dead, wounded or missing, thirty-three in one bad ambush alone in the Central Highlands which I only survived myself along with two others by playing dead.

So, I discovered what war was all about – or at least war in Vietnam. Not set-piece battles, not trumpets on the wind, no distant drum to stir the heart. It was savage street fighting in Saigon during the *Tet* offensive. It was the swamps of the Mekong Delta, the jungles of the Central Highlands, leg ulcers that ate their way through to the bone like acid and leeches that fastened on to your privates and could only be removed with the lighted end of a cigarette.

In a word, it was survival and I became rather an expert in that particular field, came through it all without a scratch until the day I was taking part in a routine search and destroy patrol out of Din To and was careless enough to step on a *punji* stake, a lethal little booby trap much favoured by the Viet Cong. Fashioned from bamboo, needle-sharp, stuck upright in the ground amongst the elephant grass and smeared with human excrement, it was guaranteed to produce a nasty, festering wound.

It put me in hospital for a fortnight and a week's leave to follow, which brought me directly to that fateful day in Pleikic when I shambled around in the rain, trying to arrange some transportation to Din To where I had to rejoin my unit. I managed to thumb a lift in a Medevac helicopter that was flying in medical supplies – the worst day's work in my life.

We were about fifty miles out of Din To when it happened, flying at a thousand feet over paddy fields and jungle, an area stiff with Viet Cong and North Vietnamese regular troops.

A flare went up suddenly about a quarter of a mile to the east of us. There was the burnt-out wreck of a small Huey helicopter in the corner of a paddy field and the man who waved frantically from the dyke beside it was in American uniform.

When we were about thirty feet up, a couple of heavy machine guns opened up from the jungle no more than fifty yards away and at that range they couldn't miss. The two pilots were wearing chest protectors, but it didn't do them any good. I think they must have both died instantly. Certainly the crew chief did, for standing in the open doorway in his safety belt, he didn't have a chance.

The only surviving crew member, the medic, was huddled in the corner, clutching a bloody arm. There was an MI6 in a clip beside him. I grabbed for it, but at the same moment the aircraft lifted violently and I was thrown out through the open door to fall into the mud and water of the paddy field below.

The helicopter bucked twenty or thirty feet up into the air, veered sharply to the left and exploded in a great ball of fire, burning fuel and debris scattering like shrapnel.

I managed to stand, plastered with mud and found myself looking up at the gentleman on the dyke who was pointing an AK47 straight at me. It was no time for heroics, especially as forty or fifty North Vietnamese regular troops swarmed out of the jungle a moment later.

The Viet Cong would have killed me out of hand, but not these boys. Prisoners were a valuable commodity to them, for propaganda as well as intelligence purposes. They marched me into the jungle surrounded by the whole group, everyone trying to get in on the act.

There was a small camp and a young officer who spoke excellent English with a French accent and gave me a cigarette. Then he went through my pockets and examined my documents.

Which was where things took a more sinister turn. In action, it was the practice to leave all personal papers at base, but because I had only been in transit after medical treatment, I was carrying everything, including my British passport.

He said slowly, 'You are English?'

There didn't seem to be much point in denying it. 'That's right. Where's the nearest consul?'

Which got me a fist in the mouth for my pains. I thought they might kill me then, but I suppose he knew immediately how valuable a piece of propaganda I would make.

They kept me alive – just – for another fortnight until they found it possible to pass me on to a group moving north for rest and recuperation.

And so, at last, I came to Tay Son. The final landing place of my jump from that railway bridge into darkness, a year and a half before.

My first sight of it was through rain at late evening as we came out of a valley – a great, ochre-painted wall on the crest above us.

I'd seen enough Buddhist monasteries to recognise it for what it was, only this one was different. A watch tower on stilts at either side of the main gate, a guard in each with a heavy machine gun. Beyond, in the compound, there were several prefabricated huts.

Having spent three days stumbling along on the end of a rope at the tail of a column of pack mules, I had only one aim in life which was to find a corner to die in. I tried to sit and someone kicked me back on my feet. They took the mules away, leaving only one guard for me. I stood there, already half-asleep, the rain drifting down through the weird, half-light that you get in the highlands just before dark.

And then an extraordinary thing happened. A man reported dead by the world's press came round the corner of one of the huts with three armed guards trailing behind him, a black giant in green fatigues and jump boots, Chaka, King of the Zulu nation, alive and shaking the earth again.

Brigadier-General James Maxwell St Claire, the pride of the Airborne, one of the most spectacular figures thrown up by the army since the Second World War. A legend in his own time – Black Max.

His disappearance three months earlier had

provoked a scandal that had touched the White House itself for, as a Medal of Honour man, he had been kept strictly out of the line of fire since Korea, had only found himself in Vietnam at all as a member of a fact-finding commission reporting directly to the president himself.

The story was that St Claire was visiting a forward area helicopter outfit when a red alert went up. One of the gun ships was short of a man to operate one of its door-mounted M60's. St Claire, seizing his chance of a little action, had insisted on going along. The chopper had gone down in flames during the ensuing action.

He changed direction and crossed the compound so briskly that his guards were left trailing. Mine presented his AK and St Claire shoved it to one side with the back of his hand.

I came to attention. He said, 'At ease, soldier. You know me?'

'You inspected my outfit at Din To just over three months ago, sir.'

He nodded slowly. 'I remember and I remember you, too. Colonel Dooley pointed you out to me specially. You're English. Didn't I speak to you on parade?'

'That's right, General.'

He smiled suddenly, my first sight of that famous St Claire charm and put a hand on my shoulder. 'You look bushed, son. I'll see what I can do, but it won't be much. This is no ordinary prison camp. The Chinese run this one personally. Forcing house number one. The commander is a Colonel Chen-Kuen, one of the nicest guys you ever met in your life. Amongst other things, he's got a Ph.D. in psychology from London University. He's here for one reason only. To take you apart.'

There was an angry shout and a young officer appeared from the entrance of one of the huts. He pulled out an automatic and pointed it at St Claire's head.

St Claire ignored him. 'Hang on to your pride, boy, you'll find it's all you have.'

He went off like a strong wind and they had to run to keep up with him, the young officer cursing wildly. Strange the sense of personal loss as I found myself alone again but I was no longer tired – St Claire had taken care of that at least.

They left me there for another hour, long

enough for the evening chill to eat right into my bones and then a door opened and an n.c.o. appeared and called to my guard who kicked my leg viciously and sent me on my way.

Inside the hut, I found a long corridor, several doors opening off. We stopped at the end one and after a while it opened and St Claire was marched out. There was no time to speak for a young officer beckoned me inside.

The man behind the desk wore the uniform of a colonel in the Army of the People's Republic of China, presumably the Chen-Kuen St Claire had mentioned.

The eyes lifted slightly at the corners, shrewd and kindly in a bronzed healthy face and the lips were well-formed and full of humour. He unfolded a newspaper and held it up so that I could see it. The *Daily Express* printed in London five days earlier according to the date. *English war hero dies in Vietnam.* The headline sprawled across the front page.

I said 'They must have been short of news that day.'

His English was excellent. 'Oh, I don't think

so. They all took the story, even *The Times*.' He held up a copy. 'They managed to get an interview with your grandfather. It says here that the general was overwhelmed by his loss, but proud.'

I laughed out loud at that one and the colonel said gravely, 'Yes, I found that a trifle ironic myself when one considers his intense dislike of you. Almost pathological. I wonder why?'

A remark so penetrating could not help but chill the blood, but I fought back. 'And what in hell are you supposed to be – a mind reader?'

He picked up a manilla file. 'Ellis Jackson from birth to death. It's all there. We must talk about Eton some time. I've always been fascinated by the concept of the place. The Sandhurst affair was certainly a great tragedy. You got the dirty end of the stick there.' He sighed heavily, as if feeling the whole thing personally and keenly. 'In my early years as a student at London University, I read a novel by Ouida in which the hero, a Guards officer in disgrace, joins the French Foreign Legion. Nothing changes, it appears.'

'That's it exactly,' I said. 'I'm here to redeem the family honour.'

'And yet you hated the idea of going into the army,' he said. 'Hated anything military. Or is it just your grandfather you hate?'

'Neat enough in theory,' I said. 'On the other hand, I never met anyone yet who had a good word for him.'

I could have kicked myself at the sight of his smile, the satisfaction in his eyes. Already I was telling him things about myself. I think he must have sensed what was in my mind for he pressed a button on the desk and stood up.

'General St Claire spoke to you earlier, I believe?'

'That's right.'

'A remarkable man – gifted in many directions, but arrogant. You may share his cell for a while.'

'An enlisted man with the top brass. He might not like that.'

'My dear Ellis, our social philosophy does not recognise such distinctions between human beings. He must learn this. So must you.'

'*Ellis*.' It gave me a strange, uncomfortable

feeling to be called by my Christian name. Too intimate under the circumstances, but there was nothing I could do about it. The door opened and the young officer entered.

Chen-Kuen smiled amicably and put a hand on my shoulder. 'Sleep, Ellis – a good, long sleep and then we speak again.'

What was it St Claire had said of him? *One of the nicest guys you've ever met?* The father I'd never known perhaps and my throat went dry at the thought of it. Deep waters certainly – too damned deep and I turned and got out of there fast.

During the journey to Tay Son, we had made overnight stops twice at mountain villages. I had been put on display, a rope around my neck, as an example of the kind of mad-dog mercenary the Americans were using in Vietnam, a murderer of women and children.

It almost got me just that, the assembled villagers baying for my blood like hounds in full cry and each time, the earnest young officer, a dedicated disciple of Mao and Uncle Ho, intervened on my behalf. I must survive to learn the error of my ways. I was a typical product of the capitalist imperialist tradition. I must be helped. Simple behaviourist psychology, of course. The blow followed by kindness so that you never knew where you were.

Something similar happened on leaving Colonel Chen-Kuen's office. I was marched across the compound to one of the huts which turned out to be the medical centre.

The young officer left me in charge of a guard. After a while, the doctor appeared, a small, thin woman in an immaculate white coat with steel spectacles, a face like tight leather and the smallest mouth I've ever seen in my life. She bore an uncanny resemblance to my grandfather's housekeeper during my early childhood, a little, vinegary lowland Scot who had never been able to forgive John Knox and therefore hated all things male. I could taste the castor oil for the first time in years and shuddered.

She sat down at her desk and the door opened again and another woman entered. A different proposition entirely. She was one of those women whose sensuality was so much a part of her that even the rather unflattering tunic and skirt of her uniform, the knee-length leather boots, could not hide it.

Her hair was jet black, parted in the centre, worn in two plaits wound into a bun at the back in a very Eastern European style, which wasn't surprising in view of the fact that her mother, as I discovered later, was Russian.

The face was the face of one of those idols to be seen in temples all over the East. The Earth Mother who destroys all men, great, hooded, calm eyes, wide, sensual mouth. One could strive on her forever, seeking the sum total of all pleasures and finding, in the end, that the pit was bottomless.

She had only the slightest of accents and her voice was indescribably beautiful. 'I am Madame Ny. I am to be your instructor.'

'Well, I don't know what that's supposed to mean,' I said, 'But it sounds nice.'

The old doctor spoke to her in Chinese. Madame Ny nodded. 'You will undress now, Mr Jackson. The doctor wishes to examine you.'

I was so tired that undressing was an effort,

but I finally made it down to my underpants. The doctor glanced up from a file she was examining, frowned in exasperation.

Madame Ny said, 'Everything, please, Mr Jackson.'

I tried to keep it light. 'Even the Marine Corps let you keep this much on.'

'You are ashamed to be seen so and by a doctor?' She seemed genuinely surprised. 'There is nothing obscene in the human form. A most unhealthy attitude.'

'That's me,' I said. 'Cold showers just never seemed to work.'

She leaned down to speak to the doctor and again they examined a file between them, presumably mine.

I peeled off like a good boy and waited. I must have stood there for twenty minutes or more and during that time various individuals, both men and women, came and went with files and papers. A study in conscious humiliation.

When it had presumably been judged I'd been punished enough, the doctor stood up abruptly and went to work. She gave me a thorough and competent examination, I'll say that for her, even to the extent of taking blood and urine samples.

Finally, she pulled forward a chair, sat down and proceeded to examine my genitals with scrupulous efficiency. It was the kind of free-from-infection check that soldiers the world over get every few months. That didn't make it any easier to take, especially with Madame Ny standing at her shoulder and following every move.

I squirmed, mainly at the old girl's rough handling and Madame Ny said softly, 'You find this disturbing, is it not so, Mr Jackson? A basic, clinical examination carried out by a woman old enough to be your mother and yet you find it shameful.'

'Why don't you jump off?' I told her.

Her eyes widened as if gaining sudden insight. 'Ah, but I see now. Not shameful, but frightening. You are afraid in such situations.'

She turned, spoke to the old doctor who nodded and they walked out on me before I could say a word. I wasn't tired any more but I found it difficult to think straight. I felt as angry and frustrated as any schoolboy, humiliated before the class for no good reason.

I had just struggled back into my clothes when Madame Ny returned with the young officer. She had a paper in her hand which she placed on the desk.

She picked up a pen and offered it to me. 'You will sign this now, please.'

There were five foolscap pages, closely typed and all in Chinese. 'You'll have to read the small print for me,' I told her. 'I haven't got my spectacles with me.'

'Your confession,' the young officer cut in. 'A factual account of your time in Vietnam as an English mercenary lured by the Americans.'

I told him what to do with the paper in an English phrase so vulgar that he obviously didn't understand. But Madame Ny did.

She smiled faintly. 'A physical impossibility, I fear, Mr Jackson. You will sign in the end, I assure you, but we have plenty of time. All the time in the world.'

She left again and the young officer told me to follow him. We crossed the compound through the rain and entered the monastery itself, a place of endless passages and worn stone steps although, surprisingly, lit by electricity.

The passage we finally turned into was obviously at the highest level, so long it faded into darkness; and, quite plainly, I heard a guitar.

As we advanced, the sound became even plainer and then someone started to sing a slow blues in a deep, mellow voice that reached out to touch everything around.

'Now gather round me people,
Let me tell you the true facts.
That tough luck has struck me
And the rats is sleeping in my hat.'

The door had two guards outside and was of heavy black oak. The young officer produced a key about twelve inches long to unlock it and it took both hands to turn.

The room was surprisingly large and lit by a single electric bulb. There was a rush mat on the stone floor and two wooden cots. St Claire sat on one of them a guitar across his knees.

He stopped playing. 'Welcome to Liberty Hall, Eton. It isn't much, but it's the London

Hilton compared to most of the accommodation around here.'

I don't think I've ever been happier to see anyone in my life.

He produced a pack of American cigarettes. 'You use these things?'

'Officer's stock?' I said.

He shook his head. 'They're being nice to me at the moment. They might give me a pack a day for a whole month, or simply cut off the supply from tomorrow morning.'

'Pavlovian conditioning?'

'That's it exactly. They have one set idea and you better get used to it. To drive you to the edge of insanity, to tear you apart, then they'll put you together again in their image. Even their psychology is Marxian. They believe each of us has his thesis, his positive side and his antithesis, the dark side of his being. If they can find out what that is, they encourage its growth until it becomes the strongest part of your nature. Once that happens, you begin to doubt every moral or decent worthwhile thing you've been taught.'

'They don't seem to be getting very far with you.'

'You could say I'm inclined to be set in my ways.' He smiled. 'But they're still trying and my instructor is the best. Chen-Kuen himself. That's just another name for interrogator, by the way.'

'I've already met mine,' I said and told him about Madame Ny and what had happened at the medical centre.

He listened intently and shook his head when I was finished. 'I've never come across her myself, but then you won't have contacts with many people at all. I haven't met another prisoner face-to-face since I've been here. Even the sessions in the Indoctrination Centre, where they feed you Chinese and Marxism by the hour, are all strictly private. You sit in an enclosed booth with headphones and a tape recorder.'

I made the obvious point. 'If what you're saying is true, why have they put me in with you?'

'Search me.' He shrugged. 'First I knew was when Chen-Kuen called me in, told me every last damn thing about you there was to know and said you'd be joining me.'

'But there must be a purpose?'

'You can bet your sweet life there is. Could be he just wants to observe our reactions. Two rats in a cage. That's all we are to him.'

I kicked a chair out of the way, walked to one of the tiny windows and stared out into the rain.

St Claire said softly, 'You're too up-tight, son. You'll need to cool it if you're going to survive round here. The state you're in now, you'd crack at the first turn of the screw.'

'But not you,' I said. 'Not Black Max.'

He was off the bed and I was nailed to the wall. The face was devoid of all expression, carved from stone, the face of a man who would kill without the slightest qualm, had done so more times than he could probably remember.

He said very slowly in a voice like a cut-throat razor, 'They have a room down below here they call the Box. I could tell you what it's like, but you wouldn't begin to understand. They locked the door on me for three weeks and I walked out. Three weeks of being back in the womb and I walked out.'

He released me and spun around like a kid,

arms outstretched, smiling like the sun breaking through after rain.

'Jesus, boy, but you should have seen their faces.'

'How?' I said. 'How did you do it?'

He tossed me another cigarette. 'You've got to be like the Rock of Gibraltar. So sure of yourself that nothing can touch you.'

'And how do you get like that?'

He lay back, head pillowed on one arm. 'I did a little *judo* at Harvard when I was a student. After the war, when I was posted to Japan with the occupation army, I took it further, mainly for something to do. First I discovered *karate*, then a lethal little item called *aikido*. I'm black belt in both.'

It was said casually, a statement of fact, no particular pride in the voice at all.

'And then a funny thing happened,' he continued. 'I was taken to meet an old Zen priest, eighty or ninety years old and all of seven stone. The guy who took me was a *judo* black belt. In the demonstration that followed, the old man remained seated and he attacked him from the rear.'

'What happened?'

'The old man threw him time and time again. He told me afterwards that his power came from the seat of reflex control, what they call the *tanden* or second brain. Usually developed by long periods of meditation and special breathing exercises. It's all just a Japanese development of the ancient Chinese art of Shaolin Temple Boxing and even that was imported from India with Zen Buddhism.'

He was beginning to lose me. 'Just how far did you go with all this stuff yourself?'

'Zen Buddhism, Confucianism, Taoism. I've boned up on them all. Studied Chinese Boxing in every minute of my spare time for nearly four years at a Zen monastery about forty miles out of Tokyo in the mountains. I thought I knew it all when I started and found I knew nothing.'

'And what's it all come down to?'

'Ever read the *Daw-Der-Jung* by Lao Tzu, the Old Master?' He shrugged. 'No, I guess you wouldn't. He says, amongst other things, that when one wishes to expand one must first contract. When one wishes to rise, one must first fall. When one wishes to take, one must first give.

Meekness can overcome hardness and weakness can overcome strength.'

'And what in the hell is all that supposed to add up to?'

'You've got to be able to relax completely, just like a cat. That way you develop *ch'i*. It's a kind of intrinsic energy. When it's accumulated in the *tan t'ien,* a point just below the navel, it has an elemental force greater than any physical strength can hope to be. There are various breathing exercises which can help you along the way. A kind of self-hypnotism.'

He proceeded to explain one in detail and the whole thing seemed so ridiculous that for the first time it occurred to me that his imprisonment might have affected him for the worst.

I suppose it must have shown on my face for he laughed out loud. 'You think I'm crazy, don't you? Well, not yet, boy. Not by a mile and a half. You listen to me and maybe you stand a ten percent chance of getting through this place in one piece. And now I'd get some sleep if I were you while you've got the chance.'

He dismissed me by picking up a book, a paperback edition of *The Thoughts of Mao*

Tse-tung. By then, I was past caring about anything. Even the short walk to my bed was an effort.

But the straw mattress seemed softer than anything I had ever known, the sensation of easing aching limbs almost masochistic in the pleasure it gave. I closed my eyes, poised on the brink of sleep and started to slither into darkness, all tension draining out of me. A bell started to jangle somewhere inside my head, a hideous frightening clamour that touched the raw nerve endings like a series of electric shocks.

I was aware of St Claire's warning cry and the door burst open and the young officer who had delivered me re-appeared, a dozen soldiers at his back and three of them with bayonets fixed to their AKs. They pinned St Claire to the wall, roaring like a caged tiger. The others were armed only with truncheons.

'Remember what I told you, boy,' St Claire called and then I was taken out through the door on the run and helped on the way by the young officer's boot.

I was kicked and beaten all the way along the passage and down four flights of stone stairs, ending up in a corner against a wall, cowering like an animal, arms wrapped around my head as some protection against those flailing truncheons.

I was dragged to my feet, half-unconscious, the clothes stripped from my body. There was a confusion of voices then an iron door clanged shut and I was alone.

It was like those odd occasions when you awaken to utter darkness at half-past three in the morning and turn back fearfully to the warmth of the blankets, filled with a sense of dreadful unease, of some horror beyond the understanding crouched there on the other side of the room.

Only this was for always, or so it seemed. There were no blankets to turn into. Three weeks St Claire had survived in here. *Three weeks*. Eternity could not seem longer.

I took a hesitant step forward and blundered into a stone wall. I took two paces back, hand outstretched and touched the other side. Three cautious paces brought me to the rear wall. From there to the iron-plated door was four more.

A stone womb. And cold. Unbelievably cold. A trap at the bottom of the door opened, yellow light flooding in. Some sort of metal pan was pushed through and the trap closed again.

It was water, fresh and cold. I drank a little, then crouched there beside the door and waited.

I managed to sleep, probably for some considerable period, which wasn't surprising in view of what I had been through and awakened slowly to the same utter darkness as before.

I wanted to relieve myself badly, tried hammering on the door with no effect whatsoever and was finally compelled to use one of the corners which was hardly calculated to make things any more pleasant.

How long had it been? Five hours or ten? I sat there listening intently, straining my ears for a sound that would not come and suddenly it was three-thirty in the morning again and it was waiting for me over there in the darkness, some nameless horror that would end all things.

I felt like screaming. Instead, I started to fight back. First of all I tried poetry, reciting it out loud, but that didn't work too well because my voice seemed to belong to someone else which made me feel more alarmed than ever. Next, I tried working my way through books I'd read. Good, solid items that took plenty of time. I did a fair job on *Oliver Twist* and could recite *The Great Gatsby* almost word-for-word anyway, but I lost out on *David Copperfield* half-way through.

It was about then that I found myself thinking about St Claire for he was already a kind of mythical hero figure as far as the American Airborne forces were concerned. St Claire and his history were as much a part of recruit training as practising P.L.F.s or learning how to take an M16 to pieces and putting it together again blindfold.

Brigadier-General James Maxwell St Claire, himself alone from the word go. Son of a Negro millionaire who'd made his first million out of insurance and had never looked back. No silver spoon, just eighteen carat gold. Harvard – only the best – and then he'd simply walked out and joined the paratroops as a recruit back in nineteen forty-one.

Captured in Italy in forty-three, as a sergeant, he'd escaped to fight with Italian partisans in the Po marshes, ending up in command of a force of four hundred that fought a German infantry division to a standstill in three days. That earned him a field commission and within a year he was captain and dropping into Brittany a week before D-day with units of the British Special Air Service.

He'd earned his Medal of Honour in Korea in nineteen fifty-two. When a unit of Assault Engineers had failed to blow a bridge the enemy were about to cross in strength, St Claire had gone down and blown it up by hand, himself along with it. By then no one in the entire American Army was particularly surprised when he was fished out of the water alive.

And his appetite for life was so extraordinary. Women, liquor and food in that order, but looking back on it all now, I see that above all, it was action that his soul craved for and a big stage to act on.

God, but I was cold and shaking all over, my

limbs trembling uncontrollably. I wrapped my arms around myself and hung on tight, not that that was going to do me much good. I think it was then that I remembered what St Claire had said, recalled even a line or two of some Taoist poem he had quoted. *In motion, be like water, at rest like the mirror.*

I had nothing to lose, that was for certain, so I sat crosslegged and concentrated on recalling every step of the breathing exercises he had described to me. His method of developing this mysterious *ch'i* he had talked about.

I tried to relax as much as possible, breathing in through the nose and out through the mouth. I closed my eyes, not that it made much difference, and covered my right ear with my left hand. I varied this after five minutes by covering my left ear with my right hand. After a further five minutes, I covered both ears, arms crossed.

It was foolishness of the worst kind, even if it was a technique a couple of thousand years old according to St Claire, but at least my limbs had stopped shaking and the sound of the breathing was strangely peaceful. I was no longer conscious of the stone floor or of the cold, simply floated there in the cool darkness, listening to my breathing.

It was like the sea upon the shore, a whisper through leaves in a forest at evening, a dying fall. Nothing.

They had me in there for eight days during which time I grew progressively weaker. Using St Claire's technique, I slid into a self-induced trance almost at will, coming out of it, as far as I could judge afterwards, at fifteen or twenty hour intervals.

During the whole period no one appeared, no one spoke. I never again saw the small trap in the door open although I did discover several more containers of water, presumably pushed through while I was in a trance. There was never any food.

Towards the end, conditions were appalling. The place stank like a sewer for obvious reasons and I was very weak indeed – very light-headed. And I was never conscious of dreaming, of thinking of anything at all, except at the very end of things when I experienced one of the most vivid and disturbing dreams of my life.

I was lying naked on a small bed and it was not dark. I was no longer in the Box for I could see again, a pale, diffused golden glow to things that was extraordinarily pleasant. It was warm. I was cocooned in warmth which was hardly surprising for the room was full of steam.

A voice called, slightly distorted, like an echo from far away. 'Ellis? Are you there, Ellis?'

I raised my head and saw Madame Ny standing no more than a yard away from me. She was wearing her uniform skirt and the leather boots, but had taken off her tunic. Underneath, she was wearing a simple white cotton blouse.

The blouse was soaking up the steam like blotting paper and as I watched, a nipple blossomed on the tip of each breast and then the breasts themselves materialised as if by magic as the thin material became saturated.

It was one of the most erotic things I have ever seen in my life, electrifying in its effect and my body could not help but respond. She came over beside the bed, leaned down and put a hand on me.

I tried to push her away and she smiled gently and said, still in that distorted, remote voice, 'But there's nothing to be ashamed of, Ellis. Nothing to fear.'

She unfastened the zip at the side of her uniform skirt and slipped out of it. Underneath she was wearing a pair of cotton pants as damp with steam as the blouse. She took them off with a complete lack of concern, then sat on the edge of the bed and unbuttoned the blouse.

Her breasts were round and full, wet with moisture from the steam, incredibly beautiful. I was shaking like a leaf in a storm as she reached out and pulled my face against them.

'Poor Ellis.' The voice echoed into the mist. 'Poor little Ellis Jackson. Nobody loves him. Nobody.' And then she pushed me away so that she could look into my face and said, 'But I do. I love you, Ellis.'

And then she rolled on to her back, the thighs spreading to receive me and her mouth was all the sweetness in life, the fire of my climax such a burning ecstasy that it had me screaming out loud.

I came awake to that scream in the darkness of the Box again, the stench of the place in my nostrils and for some reason found myself standing up straight and screaming out loud again, a blank defiance at the forces ranged against me.

There was a rattle of bolts and a moment later, the door opened and a great shaft of yellow light flooded in.

They were all there, the young officer and his men and Colonel Chen-Kuen, Madame Ny at his shoulder, very correct in full uniform including a regulation peaked cap with a red star in the front. She looked white and shocked. No, more than that – distressed, but not Chen-Kuen. He was simply interested in how well I'd stood up to things, the complete scientist.

I stood swaying from side-to-side while they busied themselves with a door next to mine. When it swung open, there was only darkness inside and then St Claire stepped out.

He had a body on him like the Colossus of Rhodes, hewn out of ebony, pride in his face as he stood there, his nakedness not concerning him in the slightest. He caught sight of me and his eyes widened. He was across the passage in two quick strides, an arm about me as I reeled.

'Not now, Ellis – not now you've got this far,' he said. 'We walk to the medical centre on our own two feet and shag this lot.'

Which gave me the boost I needed, that and the strength of his good right arm. We made it under our own steam, out through the main entrance, crossed the compound to the medical hut through a thin, cold rain falling through the light of late evening.

Once there, they parted us and I found myself alone in a small cubicle wrapped in a large towel after a warm shower. The old doctor appeared, gave me a quick check, then an injection in my right arm and left.

I lay there staring up at the ceiling and the door clicked open. It was a day for surprises. Madame Ny appeared at the side of the bed. There were tears in her eyes and she dropped to her knees beside the bed and reached for my hand.

'I didn't know they would do that, Ellis. I did not know.'

For some obscure reason I believed her, or perhaps it didn't really matter to me any more, but in any event, I have never felt comfortable in the presence of a woman's tears.

I said, 'That's all right. I made it in one piece, didn't I?'

She began to cry helplessly, burying her face against my chest. Very gently, I started to stroke her hair.

The weeks that followed had a strange, fantasy air to them and things dropped into a routine. I still shared the room with St Claire and each morning at six o'clock we were taken together to the Indoctrination Centre. Once there, we were separated to sit in small, enclosed booths in headphones, listening to interminable tapes.

The indoctrination stuff was mainly routine. Marx and Lenin to start with, then Mao Tse-tung until the old boy was pouring out of our ears. None of it ever really got through to me although I have noticed in later years that I have a pronounced tendency to argue in most situations using Marxian terminology. St Claire was a great help to me in this respect. It was he who pointed out the real and tangible flaws in Mao's works. For example, that everything he had written on warfare was lifted without acknowledgement from Sun Tzu's *The Art of War* written in 500 B.C. As the Jesuits have it, one corruption is all corruption and I could never again accept any of the great man's writings at face value.

Five hours a day were devoted to learning Chinese. In one of many interviews with me, Chen-Kuen told me that this was to help promote a closer understanding between us, an explanation which never made much sense to me. On the other hand, languages were something I'd always been good at and it gave me something to do.

Each afternoon I had a long session of 'instruction' with Madame Ny which St Claire made me report in detail to him each night, although that was only one of our activities.

He taught me *karate* and *aikido*, subjected me to lengthy and complicated breathing exercises, all designed to make me fit enough to face up to the day when we were going to crash out of there, his favourite phrase.

But he was the original polymath. Philosophy, psychology, military strategy from Sun Tzu and Wu Ch'i to Clausewitz and Liddell Hart, literature, and poetry in particular, for which he had a great love. He insisted that we talked in Chinese and even gave me lessons on his guitar.

Every minute had to be filled to use up as much as possible of that burning energy. He was like a caged tiger waiting his chance to spring.

I once tried to sum him up and could only come up with words like witty, attractive, brave, totally unscrupulous, amoral. All I know, and still believed at the end of things, was that he was the most complete man I have ever known. If anyone ever lived with total spontaneity, bringing it right up from the core of his being, it was he.

* * *

My relationship with Madame Ny was perhaps the strangest part of the whole affair.

I was taken to her office in a room on the second floor of the monastery each afternoon. There were always two guards in the corridor, but inside, we were quite alone.

It was a comfortable room, surprisingly so, although I suspect now that was mainly by design. Chinese carpets on the floor, a modern desk and swivel chairs, a filing cabinet, water colours on the wall and a very utilitarian looking psychiatrist's couch in black leather.

It became very plain from the beginning that these were psycho-analytical sessions. That she was out to strip me to the bone.

Not that I objected, for it quickly became a game of question and answer – my kind of answer – that I rather enjoyed playing and the truth is that I wanted to be with her. Looked forward to being in her company.

From the beginning, she was calm and a little remote, insisted on calling me Ellis, yet never by any remark or action, referred to that emotional breakdown at my bedside on the evening they had released me from the Box.

What I could not erase from my mind was the memory of that strange dream, an erotic fantasy so real that to see her simply get up and stretch or stand at the window, a hand on her hip, was enough to send my pulse up by a rate of knots.

A great deal of her questioning, I didn't mind. Childhood and my relationship with my grandfather, schooling, particularly the years at Eton which seemed to fascinate her. She seemed surprised that the experience hadn't turned me into a raving homosexual and asked searching and vaguely absurd questions about masturbation which only succeeded in bringing out the comic in me.

We spent a month in this way and it became obvious to me that she was becoming more and more impatient. One day she stood up abruptly after one particularly feeble joke, took off her tunic and walked to the window where she stood in the pale sunshine, angrier than I had ever seen her.

From that angle, half-turned away from me, it became obvious that her breasts managed very well without the benefit of such a western appurtenance as a brassière and I could see the line of them sloping to the nipples as the sunlight filtered through the thin cotton.

'All men are at least three people, Ellis,' she said. 'What they appear to be to others, what they think they are and what they really are. Your great fault is to accept people at face value.'

'Is that a fact?' I said mockingly.

She turned on me in anger, made a visible effort to control it, went to the door. 'Come with me.'

We didn't go very far. Through a door at the end of the corridor which led to a gallery above what was obviously the central half of the old temple. There was a statue of Buddha at the far end, flickering candles, the murmur of voices at prayer from a group of Zen monks in yellow robes.

Madame Ny said, 'If I asked you who was the commander of Tay Son you would say Colonel Chen-Kuen of the Army of the People's Republic.'

'So what?'

'The commander is down there at this moment.'

The monks had risen to their feet, their Abbot magnificent in saffron robes at their head. He glanced up at that moment and looked straight at me before moving on. *Colonel Chen-Kuen.*

We returned to her office in silence. I sat down and she said, 'So, nothing is as it seems, not even Ellis Jackson.'

I made no reply and an orderly came in with the usual afternoon pot of China tea and tiny porcelain cups. It was unfailingly and deliciously refreshing. She passed me a cup without comment and I took the first long sip with a sigh of pleasure and knew, almost instantly, that I was in trouble.

I slipped into another slot in time, my arms seemed frozen in space. The orderly had reappeared, I seemed to see him in a distorted mirror, Madame Ny opening a drawer in the desk and taking out a case containing a row of hypodermic syringes.

Her voice came from some other place, but with surprising clarity. 'We are not making the kind of progress I would wish, Ellis, and time is limited. We must try other means. Nothing painful. Just two simple injections. First, Pentathol, what you call, mistakenly, the truth drug.' I felt no pain, no pain at all as the needle went in. 'Next, a small dose of Methedrine.'

I knew what that was. Speed, the hippies called it in New York. *Speed kills,* wasn't that the phrase?

I was floating and for a moment saw myself in the chair, Madame Ny bringing her chair round to be near me, the orderly going out, closing the door behind him. Sometimes I was conscious of what I said, sometimes the conversation seemed the murmur of the sea on a distant shore, but always I talked, and one thing above all came to me with frightening vividness, just like the dream in the Box.

Helga Jorgenson wasn't really Finnish except through her husband. Swedish by origin, she had arrived at my grandfather's house in the Chilterns during the early summer of my fourteenth year. Widowed the previous year, she was thirty-five years of age with long ash blonde hair and what seemed to my hot young mind the most voluptuous figure I had ever seen. And she was the kindest person I have ever known – always smiling, always with time for me.

We were thrown together a great deal. I'd had a bad bout of glandular fever and the doctor had thought it better that I take it easy at home for the rest of that half instead of returning to school.

It was the happiest summer of my life for by chance, my grandfather was asked by the War Department to sit on an Anglo-American mutual defence committee which took him to London frequently and finally to Washington for a month.

I taught her to ride, we played tennis and went for long, rambling walks, lay in the grass to eat our sandwiches and talked and talked in a way I hadn't been able to talk to anyone in my life before. I was at the age when the sap is rising and she was a beautiful, sensual woman in her prime, used to a man and denied one.

She was in the habit of kissing me good night with a pat on the cheek that always sent a shudder of delight through me. That and the smell of her filled my mind and bed with erotic fantasies that were perfectly normal for my age.

The Tuesday in July when disaster struck was a day of intense heat, a day of utter stillness when even the birds found difficulty in singing. Helga swung in a hammock under the beech trees in the garden in a bikini and old straw hat. I lay on the ground underneath and read, for the fourth time in a month, a book I had just discovered that summer. *The Great Gatsby* by Scott Fitzgerald.

Strange, the small things that live in memory. The ladybird on my arm, sweat on my face and when I rolled over, the sight of her body through the mesh of the hammock above me.

One arm dangled limply over the side, fingers slack. On impulse, I reached up to touch them. She was half-asleep which explained her instinctive response. The fingers tightened in mine and the stomach turned hollow inside of me, more fear than ecstasy. I got to my feet slowly, half-unwilling, pulled by the hand.

She had taken off the top half of her bikini – the heat, I suppose – and lay there, the straw hat tipped across closed eyes. A shaft of pale afternoon sun touching the breasts with fire.

I started to tremble and the ache where the

ache is bound to be in such instances, was unbearable. She smiled lazily, the eyes half-opened then widened as if she only at that moment realised what was happening.

She pulled free without embarrassment and eased up the bra, leaning forward to fasten it at the back.

'I was half-asleep.'

I was trembling visibly and noticing, she frowned in genuine concern and took my hands.

'I'm sorry,' I said for it was all I could think to say.

'But that's stupid,' she replied. 'There was nothing wrong, Ellis, nothing to be ashamed of. To be so attracted at the sight of a pretty woman is normal and healthy.'

Not that I really believed her for I had been branded clean to the bone too early and rugby and cold showers had never provided much of an answer. I searched for something to say and was saved from an unexpected source. Thunder had rumbled on the horizon of things on several occasions during the past hour and now, the heavens split wide open directly above us with a sound like the last trump and the rains came.

Helga laughed and cried above the roaring, 'Let's make a run for it, Ellis. Beat you to the house.'

She was off in a second and I slipped on starting so that she was several yards in front of me, a pale yellow flash in the grey curtain. I slipped again at the side of the drive and finally made it into the conservatory liberally splashed with mud.

'Slow coach,' she called from the landing at the top of the stairs then disappeared.

The house was quiet for it was market day and the cook had gone into town in the estate car for the afternoon. I climbed the stairs slowly, trying to catch my breath and went into her bedroom.

Helga was standing in front of the dressing table, drying her hair with a white bath towel. She turned, laughing. 'Oh, what a sight you are. Here, let me.'

She wiped the mud splashes from my body quickly then started to dry my hair, shaking her head in a kind of mock gravity. 'Poor Ellis. Poor little Ellis Jackson.'

The pale yellow bikini had tightened with the

rain so that she might have had nothing on, but it wasn't that. A kind of desperate yearning not to be poor little Ellis any more, I suppose.

I kissed her clumsily and with no finesse whatsoever. Her smile faded. She didn't look angry, only solemn.

What happened then was a product of many things and she was no more to blame than I was. The situation was against us and I think she loved me in a way. There was her own need admittedly, but also, she saw mine. That this was only a symbol. That no one had ever given me real, honest-to-God-all-the-way affection and love in my life.

She kissed me very deliberately her mouth opening like a flower so that I could feel her tongue and the ache in my groin was unbelievable.

I tried to pull away from her, but she held me close and put a hand on me very deliberately. 'There's nothing to be ashamed of. Nothing at all.'

The rest was as dreamlike and unreal as everything that had gone before. She was so gentle, so calm. She took off her bikini, dried herself, then did the same for me. I was trembling violently when she pulled me across to the bed and fell back, pillowing my face against her breasts.

'Poor Ellis. Poor little Ellis Jackson. Nobody loves him. Nobody loves him but me.'

And then her mouth fastened on mine and she opened her thighs and drew me into her and the pleasure, the terrible, aching fire that burned its way through caused me to cry out in agony.

I pushed myself up on my hands, riding her like a young bull and saw, in the triple mirror above the dressing table, three images of my grandfather standing in the open doorway, the wrath of God on his face, his favourite blackthorne in his hand.

The stick descended once, twice across my back, snapping in half as I broke free.

'You dirty little animal,' he bellowed. 'Get out! Get out!'

I cowered from his wrath, filled with such fear and shame as I had never known. Helga tried to stand. He struck her back-handed across the face.

'This is how you repay me, is it?' he shouted. 'Cuckolding me with my own grandson.'

I heard no more for he kicked me out of the door and slammed it shut. I heard the bolt click into place and crept to my room.

What happened in there, I do not know, but she left that night on the London train and I returned to Eton the following day, doctor or no doctor.

I never saw Helga again.

I was still half under the influence of the drug as I came to the end.

'Cuckolding me with my own grandson,' a voice was saying. 'Cuckolding me with my own grandson.'

Madame Ny seemed excited. She leaned close and shook me by the chin. 'This is the first time you've remembered that bit, am I right?'

I nodded and said dully, 'What does it mean?'

'That she was your grandfather's mistress. It explains everything. Her age, for example. As you said, she was no ordinary au pair girl, but a mature woman in her prime. He must have picked her very carefully. His anger was the anger of the old bull seeing a younger take what he considers to be rightfully his. He has never been able to forgive you.'

'My mouth's as dry as a bone,' I said.

'That's usual.' She poured water into a glass. 'You are not angry with me?'

I swallowed about a pint and wiped my mouth. 'Why should I be? You've taught me something in helping me to remember. Why should I be ashamed because of that old bastard?'

She said calmly, 'Your sex life has not been satisfactory, am I right?'

'Bloody awful,' I said. 'I'm attracted by anything in skirts and feel as guilty as hell about it. And my performance, I've been given to understand, is only second league variety.'

'You think this will change now?'

'You tell me. You're the expert.'

She shook her head slowly. 'No, not yet.'

I was still not quite with it as she stood up, went over to the door and locked it. She turned, the sun from the window putting gold flecks in the dark eyes and started to unbutton the cotton blouse as she walked towards me.

'Poor Ellis,' she said softly. 'Poor little Ellis

Jackson. Nobody loves him. Nobody loves him, but me.'

And when I took her, on the couch so thoughtfully provided, I was back there in the bedroom at the old house again, the rain thundering into the dry ground outside, drifting in through the open window in a fine spray. And the fear was there again, mingling with the fierce, abrasive joy, sending my heart pounding, waiting for the wrath of God to burst in through the door. But this time, there was no nemesis, no nameless terror. This time there was the most complete release I have ever known.

Madame Ny stifled a cry, presumably because of the guards and gasped my name, but the name on my lips was Helga's name and in that final moment of complete release it was Helga I had taken at last.

I did not tell St Claire. Not then, for nagging away at the back of my mind was his warning about the technique they employed. To find a man's antithesis, his weakness, that of which he was ashamed and to bring it out into the open until it became the dominant factor in his personality.

But she had not done that. She had taken an open, running sore in my personality and changed it for the good. Why, I did not know, could not even comprehend, although the events of the next few weeks led me to only one conclusion.

On the following day when I was delivered to her for my session, she was cool and correct, giving no sign of what had happened the previous day. As for me, I burned for her, it was as simple as that.

She paced the room, delivering a lecture on the Marxian dialectic with every evidence of conviction. 'You must see, Ellis,' she said. 'That it is we who will win and you who will lose. History is against you.'

I wasn't particularly interested in the march of world communism for she paused only a couple of feet away from me, a hand on the desk.

I pulled her on to my knee and kissed her hard, cupping a hand over her left breast. She pushed against me, one arm sliding behind my neck and then, abruptly, stood up and went and locked the door.

From then on, I was hooked and so was she. Each afternoon the talk grew less, the activity on the couch increased. She filled my thoughts to the extent that it interfered seriously with my ability to concentrate on anything else.

St Claire couldn't help but know that something had changed. He brought it up on several occasions, usually in a half-bantering way, but I always insisted stoutly that there was nothing wrong.

'You can't trust them,' he said fiercely. 'You realise that, don't you? Not even her.'

But I didn't believe him, went blundering on to the final bitter end and only myself to blame.

It was a hot, sultry afternoon towards the end of May, with everything waiting for the monsoon to come. She seemed curiously distant, remote and far away, even troubled, though she denied it when I asked her.

God, but it was hot, the lull before the storm and our bodies were sticky with sweat and yet she held on to me passionately asking me over and over again, eyes closed in ecstasy, if I loved her, a thing she had never done before.

She had locked the door as usual, of that I was certain, and yet I was suddenly aware of the slightest of breezes and started to turn, but too late.

A long bamboo pole, the type used as a mock sword in *kendo* fighting, tapped me gently on the shoulder. Madame Ny's eyes filled with horror and she pushed me away, hands against my chest.

Chen-Kuen stood in the centre of the room, the door open behind him, dressed in his Abbot's robe, the *kendo* pole extended. As Madame Ny stood up, I tried to get between them in some gesture of protection.

'My dear Ellis, there's no need for that,' Chen-Kuen said. 'No need at all.'

I turned to look at her. She was already into her skirt and buttoning her blouse. Her face was very calm, no passion there, no fear – *nothing*.

How foolish a man can be without his trousers. I pulled mine on, hands shaking as I fastened the belt and the truth of it all, the unavoidable fact rose in my mouth like bile.

'It was all planned,' I said. 'Every last step.'

'But of course,' she said.

And then an even more staggering thought hit me. 'The dream when I was in the Box – the steam room.'

She smiled in a kind of satisfaction and that I could not forgive. I punched her solidly in the mouth and only a fraction later, Chen-Kuen delivered a basic *do* cut to the side of my head with his wooden sword that nearly unseated my brains.

In spite of that, it took three of them to get me downstairs and out into the compound. St Claire came out of the medical centre at the same time, a single guard with him and one of my guards chose that particular moment to sink the butt of his rifle into my ribs.

I went truly crazy for a short while, a rage against everything living, turned and delivered a reverse elbow strike that splintered half his chest cage.

At least a dozen guards rushed out from the monastery entrance at Chen-Kuen's call and swarmed all over me. There was another voice, too, raised in a trumpet call as Black Max arrived, like Jove descending, to help me out.

Everything he had taught me, I used. Short, devastating screw punches that focussed the *ch'i* power so that internal organs were damaged beyond repair, edge of the hand blows that splintered bone, but it could only end in one way.

I think it was the butt of an AK47 that connected with my skull and I went down into the dust amongst the whirling feet. St Claire was still at it, I heard his voice, but then that too slipped away from me.

I came back to life in half-darkness, a little light streaming in through a barred window. I groaned, there was a sudden movement and St Claire was beside me.

'Take it easy, boy. Nice and easy.'

There was the rattle of a pan, he raised my head and I sipped a little water. My skull was twice its normal size or so was the impression.

I felt the area in question gingerly and St Claire said, 'No fracture as far as I can see.'

'Where are we?'

'A punishment cell on the ground floor. What happened up there today?'

I didn't even attempt to evade that one and told him in finest detail.

He shook his head when I was finished. 'Why in hell didn't you tell me, boy? I warned you. She wasn't liberating you. She was chaining you up tighter than ever.'

'To what end?' I demanded.

'Search me.' He shrugged. 'Not that it matters.'

I managed to sit up, aware of something in his voice. 'What's that supposed to mean?'

'One of those guards died an hour ago. Ruptured spleen.'

I took a deep breath. 'You made me too good, Max.'

'Hell, no,' he said. 'It could have been me. No way of knowing.'

I said slowly, 'Are you trying to say they might put us away for good for this one?'

'They've failed with me anyway,' he said. 'No

percentage in continuing and we're both dead already in case you've forgotten.'

We didn't get the chance to discuss the matter further for a moment or so later, the door opened and they took him away.

The young officer called us to a halt, his voice hard and flat through the rain. We stood and waited while he had a look round. There didn't seem to be much room to spare, but he obviously wasn't going to let a little thing like that worry him. He selected a spot on the far side of the clearing, found us a couple of rusting trenching shovels that looked as if they had seen plenty of service and went and stood in the shelter of the trees with two of the guards and smoked cigarettes, leaving one to watch over us as we set to work.

It wasn't going to take very long, either. The soil was pure loam, light and easy to handle because of the rain. It lifted in great spadefuls that had me knee-deep in my own grave before I knew where I was. St Claire wasn't exactly helping. He worked as if there was a bonus at the end of the job, those great arms of his swinging three spadefuls of dirt into the air for every one of mine.

The rain seemed to increase in a sudden rush that drowned all hope. I was going to die. The thought rose in my throat like bile to choke on and then it happened. The side of the trench next to me collapsed suddenly, probably because of the heavy rain, leaving a hand and part of a forearm protruding from the earth, flesh rotting from the bones.

The stench was unbelievable and I turned away blindly, fighting for air, and lost my balance, falling flat on my face. At the same moment the other wall of the trench collapsed across me.

The stink of the grave was in my nostrils, my eyes. I opened my mouth to scream and then a hand like iron fastened around my collar and dragged me free.

As I surfaced, St Claire pulled me upright one-handed, holding his trenching shovel in the other. There was something in his eyes when he asked me if I was all right, a kind of madness, and behind him, the guard ran to the edge of the trench and leaned over, shouting angrily.

St Claire swung the spade back-handed like a war-axe, the rusting edge catching the guard across the side of the neck, killing him instantly. He had the man's AK47 in his great hands before the body hit the ground, pushed it on to full automatic and fired a long burst that sent the young officer and the other two guards diving for cover.

I didn't need the shove in the back St Claire gave me, but it certainly helped me on my way. I was into the trees, head-down before the first shots whispered through the branches above my head. A moment later, I emerged into another clearing of elephant grass perhaps fifty yards wide, a dozen or more water buffalo grazing peacefully.

I hesitated and St Claire arrived in time to give me another violent push. 'Keep moving,' he cried. 'If they catch us in the open we've had it.'

He fired a couple of rounds towards the water buffalo who stampeded madly in two or three different directions and I started to run again, ploughing through the elephant grass in a straight line.

The ground on the other side sloped steeply through heavy undergrowth between the trees, a length of vines and brush that made for hard going, needle thorns tearing at my fatigues and then, the bank tilted and we went down into the river, riding a wave of loose soil.

Crossing wasn't particularly difficult. The bottom was firm and the water in no place more than chest deep. It was perhaps thirty yards wide and St Claire was across before me, simply because he could move faster. When I finally made it he was already on one knee behind a curtain of vines, covering me with the AK.

I lay there face down, choking for a minute or so and finally managed to catch my breath.

'You did fine, boy, just fine,' he said.

'They'll cut us into little pieces after this one.'

'Only if they catch us.'

'Then what are we waiting for?'

'It's a hundred and seventy miles to the demarcation line,' he said calmly. 'We aren't going to make it on one rifle and whatever's left in the magazine.'

The young officer and the other two guards arrived at the same moment a few yards down stream on the other side. They entered the water without hesitation and started to wade across.

'Now,' I whispered when they were half-way, rifles raised above their heads.

He shook his head and pushed the AK on semi-automatic. 'I want their gear. There's no telling how many rounds are left in this thing so get ready to use your hands.'

Not that there was any need. They came out of the water to a spit of sand, the officer in the lead and St Claire took all three with single shots fired so rapidly they sounded like one continuous roll.

We stripped the bodies of everything worth having. Water bottles, bayonets and rubber ponchos from the two soldiers, an AK for me, several hundred rounds of ammunition, the young officer's pistol and three grenades. They had not been carrying any rations which was hardly surprising under the circumstances, but that was the least of our worries.

When we'd got all that we needed, we threw the bodies into the river. The whole business had taken no longer than five minutes and we moved back into the shelter of the jungle.

I still couldn't take it all in, so brief had been the time lapse from the grave to life again. I leaned against a tree, shaking all over. St Claire pulled his poncho over his head and picked up his AK.

'Now hear me, boy, and hear me good,' he said. 'Because I'll only say this once. Walk, don't run, that's the first rule of the jungle. We stand a chance because of the monsoon. We keep to the high country and live off the land. Monkey and parrot make fine eating when there's nothing else to be had. Under no circumstances do we ever approach a village. Even the *montagnards* aren't to be trusted. Do as I say and you'll live. Take it any other way and you're on your own.'

'That's fine by me,' I said. 'You're the boss.'

'A hundred and seventy miles to the demarcation line.' His face cracked open into that famous St Claire smile. 'But we'll make it, boy. Thirty days at the outside.'

But he was wrong. We were in the jungle all of June and the best part of July. Fifty-two days of living like animals, of hit-and-run, of kill-or-be-killed. Fifty-two days until the Sunday afternoon near Khe Sanh when we were spotted in a clearing by a Huey helicopter flying in supplies to an A.R.V.N. strongpoint.

And so I came out of the jungle, but by no means the same man who went in.

The sound of thunder

3

Instantaneous recall, the psychologists call it – every last detail of past experience floating to the surface so that one not only remembers, one lives it again with as much reality as the day it happened.

I sat there in the chair in the cottage, the whisky glass still clutched firmly in my right hand. Sheila was standing by the window smoking a cigarette, looking out, the dog crouching at her feet.

It turned its head to look at me as I moved in the chair, got up lazily and padded towards me. Something caught at my throat, half growl, half moan of agony and the glass cracked in my hand.

The dog stopped dead in its tracks and Sheila started forward, a terrible anxiety on her face.

'Ellis, what is it?' she asked.

I got to my feet and backed away. 'Get him out of here. For God's sake, get him out of here.'

She stood there, puzzlement on her face, then moved to the kitchen door and called softly to Fritz. He went to her instantly, passed into the kitchen and she closed the door.

She crossed the room quickly, put her hands on my shoulders and pushed me down in the chair. 'It's only Fritz, Ellis,' she said calmly. 'There's nothing to worry about.'

I said, 'Fritz is dead. I saw him out there in the marsh with a bullet through his head.'

'I see,' she said. 'And when was this?'

Her calmness had the wrong kind of effect in the circumstances. I grabbed her arms above the elbows and held on tight. 'They were out there, Sheila. The Viet Cong. I saw them.'

The fear in her eyes broke through to the surface like scum on a pond, terrible to see and she struggled to free herself. 'You need another drink, Ellis. Let me get you one.'

She went into the kitchen, closing the door behind her and I sat there, suspended in that terrible dream. The slight tinkle of the extension bell on the telephone on the table by the window brought me back to reality.

To have lifted the receiver would have warned her that I was listening in. Instead, I got up and moved to the serving hatch in the wall between the sitting-room and the kitchen.

It was open perhaps half-an-inch; enough for me to see part of her face, her hand clutching the receiver. The voice was subdued and full of anxiety.

'No, I must speak to Doctor O'Hara personally. It's absolutely vital.'

Sean O'Hara. The best that Harley Street could provide. I might have known.

She said, 'Sean? This is Sheila Ward. Yes, it's Ellis. I think you should get down here right away. He's worse than I've ever known him. He came in in a terrible state just now and said he'd seen Viet Cong in the marsh. It's as if he's regressed to Vietnam.' There was a pause that seemed interminable. 'No, I'll be fine. I phoned Max St Claire earlier. He should be here soon.'

As she replaced the receiver, I kicked open the

door. The Airedale was on me in a second as she cried out, his teeth bared, muzzle an inch from my leg.

She got him by the collar and hauled him away. I said, 'So I've cracked wide open, have I? Regressed to Vietnam? Well, I'll show you! I know what I saw out there. Now I'll prove it.'

I kept a couple of shot-guns in the umbrella stand by the door. I took the 16-bore, pulled a cartridge belt over my head and was out of the front door while she was still struggling to control the dog.

Rain kicked into my face, cold and sharp. This was real, this could surely be no dream and I breathed in the damp salt air and moved along the rutted track.

They were shooting again at Shoeburyness, the quiet thunder of heavy guns just as before and I paused, a coldness passing through me that sapped that new confidence which had sent me out of the cottage with blood in my eye. Had anything happened – truly? Was it then or now?

I fought against it and succeeded for the moment. Once I had survived in country like this when other men had died. I hadn't come through the worst that Vietnam had to offer to finally go to pieces in a salt marsh on the edge of the North Sea. The dog I could not explain, did not even attempt to, but the two men. Now they *had* been real for the only other explanation was so terrible that my mind refused to contemplate it for a moment.

The 16-bore was a single barrel slide repeater and took six .662 cartridges. As lethal a weapon as you could hope for at close quarters. I loaded it quickly and left the cart track a little further on, moving along a narrow, treacherous path through the marsh. A step to one side in some places could put you into the kind of bog that would swallow you up for all time.

I had to tread softly, but not just because the going was dangerous. The wild life of the marsh lurked on every side, widgeon, mallard, wild duck and teal. Any real disturbance from me and they would rise into the rain, trumpeting their alarm to the wide world.

But then I was a part of all this; had survived

too long to be anything but cunning in the ways of the Delta country. Had survived by beating the V.C. at their own game. They were good, but not good enough. Waiting for me out there in the swamp – waiting for me to declare myself. To make a mistake, as they always did. Well, two could play at that game. I crouched down in a thicket of reeds, the 16-bore ready and waited as I had waited so many times before for a sound, the briefest of murmurs, anything to indicate an alien presence.

There was no hero's welcome when I returned from Vietnam, the climate of opinion was against it and I was weighed in the balance and found wanting along with every other mercenary who had fought in other men's wars since nineteen forty-five.

My grandfather made an attempt, for medals, I suppose, were something he could understand and I had enough of those, God knows. But it didn't work. I found an older man with moist eyes and a tendency to stare into space for lengthy periods without speaking. I left him, after ten uncomfortable days, to those better qualified to care for him than I and returned to London.

What happened then had a kind of inevitability to it. A reasonably rapid slide to nowhere with the statutory bottle of Scotch a day and by a kind of personal choice. An urge to self-destruction. Old friends, who had greeted me with something like warmth, soon learned to avoid me. Nothing, it seemed, could stop me from running head-down into nowhere.

And then Black Max re-entered my life to save me for the second time as I was sliding down the wall beside the entrance to the saloon bar of a pub at the western end of Milner Street off the King's Road, the landlord having ejected me for his good and my own.

It was raining hard and I was just beginning to go when the car swung into the kerb, an Alfa Romeo G.T. Veloce, the colour of spring daffodils. The voice calling my name was from the other end of a dark tunnel, something from dream-time.

'Ellis? Ellis, is that you?'

I opened my eyes and managed to focus with

some difficulty. He was in dress uniform, returning to his hotel – as I found later – from a reception at the American Embassy.

'It's raining, Max,' I said. 'Your medals will get rusty.'

His laughter shook the street from one end to the other. 'By God, Ellis, but it's good to see you.'

Which was exactly how I felt. Tay Son again in the rain and our first meeting. Remembering that, I started to cry helplessly like a child. I suppose it was then that he realised just how sick I was.

It was raining again now, blowing in across the marsh in a slanting curtain. Somewhere in the distance, birds lifted in alarm and I heard a car engine.

I cut through a patch of reeds and scrambled up on top of the nearest dyke. There was only one person it could be. I caught a brief glimpse of the Alfa Romeo, a smudge of yellow vivid in the grey morning as it turned off the side road into the cart track leading across the marsh.

I ran along the top of the dyke throwing caution to the winds, mainly because it took me three-quarters of the way across that section of the marsh, jumped down at the far end and ran, knee-deep through water, the 16-bore held across my chest.

I was conscious of the Alfa's engine, birds calling in alarm and then it stopped abruptly. I suppose I knew at once what had happened – knew as if the whole thing had happened before.

I came out through the reeds and found the Alfa forty yards to the right of me. One of the Viet Cong stood in the centre of the track, covering St Claire who was getting out of the car. He was in uniform and wore his own private version of a general officer's overcoat, a kind of British warm with fur collar.

He towered over his assailant and stood, hands on hips. The V.C. raised the AK threateningly. What happened then was purely reflex, the soldier's instinct for action for it seemed to me that he intended to shoot St Claire dead.

Where a man is concerned, a shot-gun is deadly up to twenty yards and I had forty to go which meant I very probably was running to my death, but at least it would give St Claire a chance to save himself, or so it seemed to me then.

I went in on the run, mouth open in a *banzai* cry savage enough to split the world in two, firing from the hip as I went.

The V.C. swung round, loosing off a quick burst, an involuntary action, his bullets raising fountains to the right of me.

It was the only chance he got for St Claire had him in an instant stranglehold from the rear, falling backwards, one knee raised to break his spine as they fell.

The other V.C. stepped out of the reeds on the far side of the Alfa. I cried a warning and loosed off another of my useless shots. St Claire rolled, grabbing for the first man's AK, firing it smoothly in the same moment, a long burst slashing through the reeds, sending the other man jumping for cover.

St Claire rolled into the ditch and stayed low. After a while, he waved and fired a quick burst into the reeds to cover me while I ran to join him. There were a couple of shots in reply, but

I made it in one piece, sliding over the edge of the ditch.

He grinned, 'For a guy who's supposed to be be coming apart at the seams, you looked pretty good out there. Just like old times.'

'Doesn't anything ever throw you?' I demanded.

'Life's too short, boy. I've told you that before.' He nodded towards the first V.C. who was lying in the middle of the track. 'Okay, sweetheart, so what are the Viet Cong doing in the Essex marshes?'

'Christ knows,' I said. 'I thought I was going out of my mind when they jumped me earlier and Sheila certainly did. That's why she phoned you. She's even got Sean O'Hara coming down at the double complete with hypo and tranquillisers.'

'So she's on her own back there?' He frowned. 'That isn't so good in the circumstances and we certainly aren't going to find the answer to this thing by hanging around here. What I need right now is a telephone.'

'So what do you suggest?'

'You get into the Alfa. Keep your head down,

but get her started. I'll give you some covering fire and we'll make a run for it.'

He moved a little way further along the ditch and fired three or four shots into the reeds on the other side of the road. I didn't wait for an answer, wasn't even sure if one came. I crawled across to the Alfa and wormed my way behind the wheel, dumping the shot-gun on the rear seat.

I shouted to St Claire, starting the engine and moving into gear at the same moment. He loosed off a long burst into the reeds and was into the passenger seat, head-down as I moved off, accelerating so sharply that the rear wheels kicked up a great curtain of mud and filth.

I went down the track at fifty miles an hour, a hair-raising speed considering the conditions, crossed the unfenced dyke over the main stream without slowing at all and skidded to a halt on the cobbled yard of the cottage within a couple of minutes of leaving the scene of the ambush.

There was no time for conversation and within a second of stopping I was out of the

Alfa and running for the door calling her name, St Claire close behind.

I don't know what happened as I went through the door for this part of the affair is not too clear to me, but I certainly went down the steps into the sitting-room head first with the appropriate result.

I came to my senses to find myself lying on the couch, though perhaps floating would be a better word for it. Once again, it was as if I was disembodied, as if nothing physical existed for me at all.

I was filled with the most dreadful nausea so that my stomach seemed to turn inside out. I rolled over, fell to the floor and was violently sick.

I lay there for a while. There was something hard underneath me, something painful and when I sat up; I found it was the 16-bore. I picked it up and used it as a prop to get upright for I found it almost impossible to keep my feet.

The door to the bedroom was open and the

light was on. I called Sheila's name or thought I did for no sound came from my mouth, then floated towards the open doorway.

Something waited for me in there, something terrible and yet it was not to be avoided and I was drawn towards the door inexorably.

The first thing I saw was the blood in a scarlet crescent splashed across the white painted wall. Sheila lay in the centre of the room, quite naked except for a sheet entwined round one leg, as if she had tripped over it while trying to run. The back of her skull had been smashed like an eggshell.

St Claire lay back across the bed, one knee raised, as naked as she except for the dog tags around his neck that he never took off, an old affectation.

Only it wasn't St Claire when I got close. It wasn't anybody, for there was no face – only the bloody pulp left by a couple of shot-gun cartridges fired at close range.

I turned to run, found myself still clutching the 16-bore and threw it away from me with a cry. There was someone standing in the doorway watching me, I knew that, but who it was impossible to say for it was as if I fainted and everything around me melted into darkness.

Once, skin-diving in Cornwall using aqualung equipment, I had valve trouble with my reserve bottle of air and only just made it to the surface in time. It was like that now, kicking hard, struggling with everything I had to rise through cold water towards a small patch of light.

I made it at last, breaking through to the surface, gasping for air, and found myself naked under an ice-cold shower, held there by a burly individual with close-cropped hair and a broken nose.

I tried to push his hands away and found there was no strength in me at all. My hands seemed to rise in slow motion, to float as if suspended in water, then to drift down again.

The man who was holding me called over his shoulder, 'Doctor, he's coming out of it.'

The voice echoed inside my head, I seemed to float over the side of the bath, which was surely impossible, and Sean O'Hara appeared in the doorway.

He was handsome enough in his own decadent Irish way with a face on him like Oscar Wilde or Nero himself and a mane of silver hair that made him look more like an actor than what he was, which was, quite simply, one of the finest psychiatrists in Western Europe.

I said, 'Now then, you old bastard. Still getting your own back on the bloody English at fifty guineas a session?'

He didn't smile, not even an attempt which was unusual for he could laugh at the drop of a hat, but then, so did everything else seem strange. Even my voice sounded as if it belonged to a stranger.

He took down my bathrobe from behind the door and held it open for me. 'Get this on, Ellis, there's a good lad and come along with me.'

I was perfectly calm, no anxiety at all, conscious of no particular feeling about anything. Simply floated, trapped in that strange, dreamlike state.

Sean waited patiently while I fiddled with the belt, then put a hand on my shoulder. 'All right, then, let's get it over.'

The sitting-room seemed crowded with people,

all men I had never seen before, two in shirt sleeves on the floor making various measurements. There was a uniformed policeman at the door, the sudden flash of a camera bulb. Everyone stopped talking.

I waited patiently while Sean and a small, brisk, dark-haired man in gold-rimmed spectacles talked in low tones then Sean turned and took my arm.

'We'll go into the bedroom now, shall we, Ellis?'

And it was waiting for me, there behind the half-open door. That nameless horror which had haunted my dreams for so many months. My throat went dry, I was conscious of my heart pounding and found it difficult to breathe. I tried to pause and Sean drew me relentlessly on.

When he pushed the door open with his foot, the first thing I saw was the blood in a great scarlet crescent splashed across the white-painted wall.

I turned, clutching at him as the earth moved. 'A dream,' I said brokenly. 'I thought it was a dream.'

'No dream, Ellis,' he said gravely. 'This happened. This has to be faced.'

He pushed me forward into the room.

They put me on a chair in the kitchen and someone produced a cup of tea. It tasted like something out of a sewer and I lurched to the sink and vomited. I turned wearily and a young constable helped me across to my chair again as Sean O'Hara and the man in the gold-rimmed spectacles appeared.

'How do you feel now, Ellis?' Sean asked.

'I'll live, I suppose.' Again, the voice seemed to come from somewhere outside me.

He produced a small white pill box from his pocket, opened it and shook three or four of the familiar purple capsules into his palm.

I told you how lethal these things can be. I gave Sheila your prescription for another twenty-one last Wednesday. From what's left in here, I calculate you must have taken ten or twelve of the bloody things earlier. If I hadn't arrived when I did, you'd be dead by now.'

'Which was presumably what Mr Jackson intended,' the man in the gold-rimmed spectacles put in. 'Isn't that so, sir?'

'As you know, this whole area is owned by the Defence Ministry.' Sean put in. 'Superintendent Dix here, of the Special Branch, is in charge of security.'

I seemed to experience some difficulty in focussing my eyes when I turned to Dix. 'What are you trying to say? That I tried to commit suicide after knocking them both off? I didn't even take those bloody pills.'

I brought out this last bit with such violence that the young constable on the door stirred uneasily.

'So you can't remember, sir?' Dix produced a tiny bottle. 'Not surprising if you were on this.'

I seemed to have moved into one of those stages when I wasn't worried again. I said, 'And what might that be?'

'L.S.D. We found it in your bedside locker.'

'Well, I've news for you,' I told him. 'I've never touched that stuff in my life.'

'We've already taken blood samples while

you were unconscious, sir. There's really no way out, you know.'

'Tell me about the Viet Cong, Ellis,' Sean said quietly.

I looked at them both, faces grave, waiting for what I had to say. Even the young constable had taken an involuntary step closer. It was then that I noticed the open door, the men outside, all waiting.

There was a new arrival, a paratroop major in the kind of uniform which had been tailored in Savile Row, red beret tilted at the exact regulation angle, a lazy, fleshy, amiable face except for the eyes which were like lumps of jagged glass. I knew him, that was the intriguing thing, but couldn't remember where from. He nodded slightly as if to encourage me.

'You think I'm mad, don't you?' I said. 'Well, they were out there and Max and I took them on. That's cold, hard fact and there's the body of the man he killed lying up there on the track to prove it.'

Dix shook his head. 'Nothing there, Mr Jackson. Not a damned thing.'

In the silence which followed I seemed to wait

for another blow from the axe. It came soon enough.

Dix said, ‘As you know, this whole area is Defence Ministry property so we check on people’s movements, regular movements, rather carefully. Mrs Ward, for instance, was in the habit of going up to London every Thursday.’

‘To see her eight-year-old son.’ I nodded. ‘She was divorced. Her husband had custody.’

He shook his head. ‘Her husband has been lecturing at the University of Southern California for the past two years, sir. There never was a son.’

I gazed at him stupidly and Sean said, ‘She spent the whole day at Max’s flat, Ellis, whenever she was in town.’

I came apart at the seams, put my head down on my folded arms and fought for survival, great waves flowing over me.

Through the roaring, I heard Sean O’Hara say, ‘Any further attempts at this stage would be quite useless. The hallucinatory state which follows L.S.D. can last for days. Typical clinical symptoms. I think we should commit him to Marsworth Hall as soon as may be and I’ll arrange for some intensive treatment. He's quite obviously a danger to himself and everyone else in his present state.'

Marsworth Hall, a staging house for Broadmoor, last stop for the criminally insane. Sean gave them a day a week as consultant free. Such interesting cases, as he had once told me. The prospect of those gates closing on me for ever was so terrible that I staggered to my feet, reaching out to him frantically.

'They were there. They did exist.'

'And Fritz?' he said gently. 'You told Sheila they shot him yet he's outside now, tied up in his kennel. Would you like to see him?'

And then I remembered – remembered the one thing that had happened which shouldn't have. A complete impossibility.

'The dog that was shot,' I cried. 'It wasn't Fritz – it couldn't have been. It jumped off the dyke and swam fifty yards through deep water.' They stared at me, puzzled. I said, 'Fritz can't swim.'

The silence which followed was like that iron gate swinging shut. Someone coughed and Dix nodded briefly.

The young constable took my arm. 'All right, sir, if you'll come with me.'

I twisted in a half-circle, broke his arm with one blow and threw him out through the door to clear a path for me. Fear – complete panic, call it what you like, but I went berserk.

They moved in on me like a rugby scrum and my bathrobe was torn off within seconds which left me naked as the day I was born. *Tom-a-Bedlam running amok*. Next came the chains.

I gave a fair account of myself, sent one man back screaming as his ribs went, broke another's jaw and then the paratroop major moved in and kicked me in the stomach, perfect *karate*, the foot flicking upwards only when the knee was waist-high.

Not that it was enough, that's what having *ch'i* does for you. I moved in on him, hands raised, remembering who he was at the same time. My first half at Eton, his last. The wall game. Hilary Vaughan, the pride of the school. Brains and brawn, poetry and boxing. No one could ever make him out, especially when he entered the army.

He knew that I had recognised him, saw it in my eyes and frowned involuntarily, as if it didn't make sense – as if it was something he hadn't expected. In any event, it was round about then that the rugby scrum won and I went down under the sheer weight.

But it took six of the bastards to get me out to the car, handcuffs or no handcuffs.

Time out of mind

4

Marsworth Hall was the kind of eighteenth century country house you seem to find in England and nowhere else. Not quite as large as Blenheim Palace, but not much smaller. There was a twenty-foot perimeter wall topped by what was very obviously a recent innovation – an electrified wire fence and we were admitted through electronically operated gates.

It was rather like Tay Son, at least in atmosphere. Dusk was falling and there was a strange lack of people. In fact, during the time I was there, I saw no other patients at all.

Sean dealt with the formalities, handing me over at once to two male nurses. They were of a type to be expected. Large, intimidating men, one with the flattened nose and scar tissue around the eyes peculiar to those who have boxed a great deal and both had the efficient, no nonsense air about them that one associates with ex-Guards' n.c.o.s.

The more reasonable of the two was called Thompson and the ex-boxer, Flattery. They took me to a shower room where I was thoroughly washed down with the aid of the usual Ministry of Works carbolic soap, then provided with pyjamas, the trousers of which had an elasticated top and there was no cord to the dressing gown.

We went up to the top floor in a small lift and Thompson unlocked a door directly opposite while Flattery clutched my arm which gave me my first real insight into the man's character. He held me in an unnecessarily vice-like grip that left the arm half-paralysed. I had thought he would be Irish but when he spoke, it was obvious that he came from Liverpool.

'In you go,' he said and gave me a shove.

It was a fine and private place, bed, wardrobe, locker, private lavatory, except when someone looked in through the spy hole in the door and there was a view of the grounds between bars.

'Now what?' I demanded.

'Now nothing.' He chuckled harshly. 'We lead a very quiet life here and we like it that way, but if you want trouble, you can have it.'

Thompson, who had looked vaguely uneasy during this speech, said in a much more conciliatory tone, 'I wouldn't get into bed yet if I were you. Dr O'Hara wants to see you before he goes.'

The door closed and I was alone, yet not alone, my mind racing in an effort to keep up with the dozens of different thoughts and images that bubbled to the surface.

I lay down on the bed and tried to relax and found it impossible for I was still subject to sudden changes in consciousness. One moment I was myself and thinking clearly and objectively again, the next, someone else entirely, outside of things, floating in a kind of hiatus, unable to make even two and two add up to four any more.

I forced myself back to that morning, starting with the dream and progressing through each incredible incident, looking for some pattern. And yet what pattern could I hope to find? If what Sean O'Hara had indicated was true, then I had never really wakened from that dream at dawn and the whole day was simply a continuation of it.

Time passed – an hour, perhaps two. I heard steps on one occasion and an eye appeared at the peephole in the door. Constant surveillance, which made sense. I had, after all, attempted suicide once that day. Even thinking about that made the hackles rise, made me feel viciously angry as if my whole being rebelled against the idea.

It was round about then that footsteps sounded outside again, the key rattled in the lock and Flattery ushered Sean O'Hara in. Sean dismissed him and stood against the closed door for a while, his face grave.

'How do you feel now, Ellis?'

'I'd say that was a reasonably stupid question.'

'Perhaps. Would you care for a cigarette?'

It tasted foul which surprised me for he only smoked a very exclusive brand of Sullivan. I made a face and stubbed the cigarette out.

He had been watching me searchingly and

nodded his head slightly. 'Only to be expected. Your whole body chemistry's up the creek.'

'And what's that supposed to mean?'

He sat on the end of the bed. 'I've just had the necessary tests run through in the lab here. Blood, urine, saliva – the usual things.'

I knew what he was going to say, of course, just by looking at him, yet had to hear the cold facts spoken out loud.

'All right, surprise me.'

'That you'd taken those capsules was something I was reasonably certain of – the tests only confirm it. I didn't want to believe in the L.S.D. bit, but that's a hard fact of life now also. How long have you been taking it?'

'You tell me.'

He got angry, the Irish in him exploding to the surface. 'God damn it, man, I've been trying to help you find yourself again for nearly a year now and not just for those bloody fees you're always cracking on about. I liked you – still do, if it comes to that. You went through an experience out there in Vietnam that would have finished most men and stayed on your own two feet. Problems, yes, but nothing we couldn't put right. But L.S.D.' He got up and moved to the window. 'Of all things for a man with your background to take, that was the worst you could have chosen. The effect on anyone suffering from even the slightest instability can be incalculable.'

I said slowly, 'Anything I could say would be a complete waste of time and energy so just tell me one thing, then go. What happens now?'

He shrugged. 'It seems there's a security element involved. Something to do with the work St Claire was doing. We'll know more tomorrow. They'll be coming to see you.'

'Superintendent Dix?'

He shook his head. 'No, it seems a Major Vaughan will be handling it. A paratroop officer but he's tied up with intelligence in some way. He was up at the cottage.'

'A good man with his boot,' I said. 'Now I think I'll go to bed, Sean. I don't think there's much more either of us can say at the moment and I'm tired.'

I turned my back on him, took off my dressing gown and climbed between the sheets. He knocked on the door and said, 'I'm afraid the light will have to be left on all night. I'm sorry about that.'

'That's all right.' I said. 'You seem to forget I'm the original expert on this kind of thing. In a manner of speaking, I've been here before.'

The door closed. I lay there staring up at the ceiling. After a while I heard the key again and Thompson entered with a half-pint mug which he put down against the wall by the door.

He smiled awkwardly. 'I thought you might like a cup of tea.'

'What's wrong?' I demanded. 'Did O'Hara warn you not to get too close? Where's your pal?'

'Flattery?' He shrugged. 'Half-way to the village by now. He likes his beer. It's his night off and you made him late which he'll hold against you. I'd watch that if I were you.'

He went out, the door closed again and for the last time that night and I was finally alone. I looked across at the mug of tea on the floor by the door. For some reason it reminded me of the Box. Tay Son all over again and I fell asleep and dreamt of Madame Ny.

* * *

Surprisingly, I slept quite well and was finally awakened at seven-thirty by Thompson and Flattery who appeared together bringing my breakfast on a tray. Porridge without cream, lukewarm scrambled egg, and cold, brittle toast. They left me to eat it and returned in a quarter of an hour and took me along to the shower room.

Lying there in bed I had somehow felt myself again, slightly light-headed, but no more than that. It was only when I got on my feet and started to walk that I realised I was still in trouble. The walls undulated slightly, the corridor stretched into infinity. There was that peculiar feeling of being somehow outside of myself again.

Yet I was still capable of rational thought or so it seemed. Still able to make some kind of judgement about things. Flattery, for example, was different – different in his attitude to me. It was as if he had been spoken to – warned off, perhaps.

Yet it was more subtle than that. There was a new interest in the way he looked at me, a kind of calculation in the eyes, I noticed that particularly, especially when I was shaving in front of a small mirror with an electric razor they provided. He watched me only when he thought I wasn't looking at him and glanced away when I did. And his hand on my arm was considerably more gentle than it had been the previous night when they took me back along the corridor.

My feet seemed to spurn the ground and I moved in slow motion, seemingly in perfect control and yet it must have showed for Thompson cried out something unintelligible, the voice distorted in an echo chamber again, and grabbed my other arm.

The lift door opened at the same moment and Sean O'Hara appeared. He took in the situation at a glance, I suppose, for I was conscious of him running forward, mouth opening and closing as if he were talking.

The next thing I knew, I was on the bed in my room, staring up at the light bulb which for some reason was the size of a balloon and then, just like that, there was a kind of click inside my head and the bulb jumped back to normal size.

Flattery waited at the door and Thompson was holding a tray for Sean who was in the act of filling a hypodermic. I struggled up and he turned instantly and moved to my side.

'Are you going to stick that thing in me or not?' I demanded.

He glanced at the hypo, smiled and dropped it into the tray Thompson held out to him. 'How do you feel?'

'A little weak, but I can think straight. For a while there, I was in that dream world again.'

He nodded gravely. 'I'm afraid this kind of thing will continue for some days. At least if you know what's happening, it won't frighten you. You're lucky. On the dosage you took, most people would either be dead now or hopelessly insane.'

'You always were a comfort.'

He smiled with something like warmth which in the circumstances surprised me. 'You'd better rest now. I don't really think you're up to interviews yet. Major Vaughan's here. He was hoping you might be in a fit state to talk to him, but I can always put him off.'

'No thanks.' I stood up. 'I'd like to get it over

with as soon as possible. I've always preferred to know the worst or had you forgotten?'

'Fair enough. By far the best way of looking at things. I'll go down now and check that he's ready for you and you can follow at your own pace with Flattery.'

Flattery's hand on my arm was still gentle and he called me sir a couple of times. Quite a turnabout. He went along the corridor past the lift and he unlocked a door at the far end and ushered me through. I found myself standing at the end of a narrow steel bridge, not much more than a catwalk that spanned the courtyard at the rear of the main block, obviously constructed to give quick access to the east wing. It was roofed with some kind of transparent plastic, but the sides were open to the four winds and protected only by a three-foot rail.

The early morning sunshine was momentarily dazzling. I averted my eyes quickly as I started to cross and got the shock of my life as St Claire's yellow Alfa Romeo turned into the courtyard sixty feet below.

I grabbed for the rail and waited, heart pounding. The door swung open, long, lovely legs, a flash of several hundred poundsworth of leopard-skin coat and then she was out clutching a formal-looking leather briefcase. Tall, proud, beautiful – skin not quite as dark as St Claire's, hair wholly Negroid and proud of it.

She glanced up casually and saw me and called my name instantly. I closed my eyes, finally convinced the whole world really had gone mad and almost went over the rail.

Helen St Claire was her brother's especial pride. Brains and beauty, he used to say, and I knew her history backwards long before I ever met her. As a medical student, prizes all along the way. After taking her M.D. she'd branched out into general psychiatry, finally specialising in behaviourist therapy with children.

But we'd never met, not until that famous occasion when St Claire had discovered me sliding down the wall of that pub in Milner Street, had re-entered my life to save it for a second time.

He was due back in Paris the following day where he was something big with NATO Intelligence Headquarters at Versailles and had insisted on taking me back with him to the apartment at Auteuil with the cantilevered terrace that hung in space over the Seine giving the kind of view of Paris that seized you by the throat.

Helen was living with him at that time – working in a children's hospital and researching for a Ph.D. at the Sorbonne in her spare time which for some reason he completely failed to mention to me. She wasn't exactly expecting me either, for when we arrived on that first night, she had just finished dressing to go out to dinner and was waiting for her escort who, when he arrived, turned out to be a seventy-year-old Austrian Professor of Chemical Psychiatry at the Sorbonne.

A fine time they had between them over me. For a month, she dropped everything, watched over me like a broody hen. Never a hope of a drink did I have until the first week was over and my system was clear of the damn stuff and I was ten years younger and eating again.

After that, another kind of therapy. Paris in depth. She arranged a careful schedule day-by-day. You name it, we saw it. Churches, galleries, every historical building worth a footnote. And in between, gay meals at pavement cafés where she drank champagne which I insisted on because I was strictly regulated to coffee, tea or mineral water. Versailles, the woods at St Germaine sheltering under a beech tree from a sudden shower.

She was a couple of years older than me, a vital, beautiful girl, utterly dedicated to her work and I was in love with her up to and including that final week of torture when St Claire had to fly to Washington unexpectedly and we were left alone. I wanted her more than I'd ever wanted any woman, a constant itch that wouldn't go away. Just to be near her was hell in a hundred subtle ways. To watch her sit down, get up, move around the place, reach for things, the skirt of a sky-blue dress she was fond of at the time sliding six inches up her thigh . . . but she was St Claire's sister. There was a kind of honour involved.

In the end, of course, my depression showed.

She came in one night and found me on drink number one, a small Scotch admittedly for by then she had established the pleasing fact that I wasn't really an alcoholic.

She asked me what was wrong and I told her, my natural tendency to over-dramatise anything bursting forth in a wonderful little scene that was as good as anything Noël Coward ever wrote. At the end, she had smiled gravely, taken my by the hand and had led me to her bedroom.

What had happened then was the greatest humiliation possible. Nothing I did, no amount of careful lovemaking, had the slightest effect on her. She caressed me in a calm, impersonal way, and certainly kissed me with considerable affection, but there was nothing else. I finally pleasured myself, if that is the word for it, and rolled off that magnificent body feeling utterly miserable.

Three nights like that was all I could take. She was beautiful, superbly intelligent and one of the most genuinely compassionate people I have ever met. Perhaps it was all sublimated so that there was nothing left over. Certainly there wasn't what I wanted, needed, if you like, as some kind of reassurance, although of what, I am not quite sure.

And so I fled from her, to London and the slippery slope. To grab at a lifeline called Sheila Ward, to decay a little bit more each day in the Foulness Marshes.

I was shown into a room on the ground floor which had obviously once been a small drawing-room and still had great style with a gilt mirror over an Adam fireplace and white and blue Wedgwood plaques on the walls.

Sean was sitting behind a modern desk. There were a couple of easy chairs, bookshelves and a row of filing cabinets, but the main incongruity was the bars at the long windows, their shadows slanting across the Chinese carpet in the pale morning sunshine.

'Yours?' I asked.

He nodded. 'Very nice, but we can't even put in an electrical plug without getting permission from the Ministry. The whole place is under some kind of preservation order.' He faltered into temporary silence and then added with some force, 'Look, I'm on your side, Ellis. All right?'

'I never doubted it.' I said. 'Now wheel him in and let's get it over with.'

I moved to the window and looked out across green lawn to a fringe of beech trees. Rooks lifted lazily in the clear air, came down again. It was all very autumnal, very English out there beyond the bars.

Hilary Vaughan said, 'Hello, Ellis, it's been a long time.'

He was still in uniform, his red beret vivid in the sunlight. He had come through a door in the panelling to one side which I had failed to notice earlier and which now stood ajar.

'A long time since what?' I asked.

'You fagged for me during my last half at Eton or had you forgotten?'

'There was an oaf called Chambers,' I said. 'Played for the first eleven. Used to take a cricket stump to us if he thought we weren't being nippy enough. You caught him giving me a thrashing one day and broke his nose.'

'He took over the family business against all

advice and went broke in three years,' he said. 'Merchant banking. He never was up to much.'

He pulled off his beret, took a file out of his briefcase and sat down at the desk. 'They shouldn't have chucked you out of the Academy.'

'It didn't exactly break my heart.'

'You never wanted to go in the first place, did you?'

'You seem to know.'

'Then why did you go to Vietnam?'

I helped myself to a cigarette from a box on the table. 'It seemed like a good idea at the time.'

He tapped one of the papers on the desk. 'This is a copy of your confidential report on file at the Pentagon, *A born soldier with outstanding qualities of leadership*. That's a direct quote. Bronze Star, Vietnamese Cross of Valour plus the D.S.C. they gave you and St Claire for escaping. That adds up to quite a record.'

'It should also read somewhere *Unfit for further service*,' I pointed out. 'Or did you miss that choice bit of information? Nutty as a fruitcake, although they put it more politely.'

'The general must have been proud of you.'

'You can stick the general where grandma had the pain.' I stubbed my cigarette out impatiently. 'What in the hell has all this got to do with what happened yesterday, anyway?'

I can see now that he was only feeling his way, had wanted to get me talking. He said, 'Okay, what *did* happen yesterday?'

'All right,' I said. 'I woke up yesterday morning, took a dose of L.S.D. large enough to kill most people so that I could have hallucinations about the Viet Cong chasing me through the marshes. This naturally led to my mistress sending a cry for help to my best friend who came galloping to the rescue, then decided to get into bed and screw her instead which left me no alternative but to blast them both and then do the only decent thing.'

He laughed, head back, his whole body shaking. 'You have a gift for the apt phrase, old lad, I'll give you that.'

He had a good face, I noticed that in an abstracted sort of way as he leaned back. Fleshy, perhaps, and there was certainly arrogance there, but it had been a mistake to think him amiable.

A soldier's face – a scholar's also and one thing was certain. Here was an utterly ruthless man. A Regency buck born out of his time. The kind who would play cards all night, find half-an-hour for his mistress then face his man at ten paces under the trees at dawn and put a bullet between his eyes.

He said casually, 'Did you know that your friend, Mrs Ward, was an active Marxist when she was an art student?' I stared at him blankly and he carried straight on. 'Those visits of hers to St Claire's place on Thursdays when he was in town – they were a fact as Dix told you last night. Do you think they were having it off?'

I stood up and walked to the window. 'I wasn't her keeper. We certainly weren't in love or anything like that. It was a kind of mutual aid society. She looked after me in her way and I looked after her in mine. If she and Max were up to anything, then it was their own business.'

'On the other hand, she could have been simply giving him progress reports on you?'

'That's possible. He worried about me.'

Vaughan looked at the paper in front of him again. 'One thing does strike me as very odd.

You come in from the marsh raving away and she immediately phones for General St Claire.'

'I've had breakdowns of one kind and another before and he's always come running,' I said. 'We had a special relationship, just like Britain and America.'

'But why did she wait so long before phoning your psychiatrist? They both had to pass through the Special Branch point at Landwich on their way to Foulness. I have the records here and Dr O'Hara was booked through an hour and a half later than the general.'

I wasn't thinking too straight and there was an ache at the back of my head which had to be felt to be believed. I said, 'Look, what in the hell are you driving at?'

He ignored my question and said instead, 'Now tell me again what happened yesterday in that damned marsh, only the truth this time or at least what you remember as the truth.'

It didn't take long and when I was finished he sat for quite some time, chin in hands. I said, 'Yes, I know, typical hallucinatory symptoms after taking L.S.D., isn't that what Sean O'Hara said?'

'But you said you didn't take L.S.D.'

'The tests he's run on me indicate otherwise. A massive dose. I'm slipping from this world into the next so often at the moment that I don't know where I am.'

'Then who gave it to you?' he cut in sharply. I stared at him blankly. 'If you didn't take it yourself, then someone administered it to you. It's quite simple. A few drops soaked into a lump of sugar. Dropped into your tea perhaps or a cup of coffee.'

I stared at him in genuine horror and he said gently, 'It had to be her, Ellis, there *is* no one else.'

He was right, of course, had to be if what I remembered was the truth of things. I said hoarsely, 'But why? Why should she do that to me?'

'You'd be surprised just how much sense this whole affair does make,' he said. 'Your story, for instance.'

I was thunderstruck. 'You mean you believe it?'

'It makes a damn sight more sense than the other one.'

'Then you also believe I didn't murder them?'

He produced from the file a photo of that body sprawled across the bed, one knee raised, face obliterated.

'Well, you certainly didn't kill St Claire, old lad.' He smiled beautifully. 'You see, that isn't him.'

Action by night

5

I grabbed at a chair to steady myself and turned it over, going down on one knee. There was a cry of alarm and Helen St Claire came in through that door in the panelling like a strong wind, Sean O'Hara a step behind her.

I managed a smile. 'I wondered who in the hell this cunning bastard had out there.'

They got me into the chair which Sean had set upright again, but she couldn't manage even the trace of a smile in return for mine. She was all worry and concern.

'Ellis, you look like hell. What did they do to you?'

'Never mind that.' I turned to Vaughan. 'What proof have you?'

'Me!' Helen cut in. 'Major Vaughan spoke to me on the phone in Paris yesterday afternoon and asked me to come as soon as possible. I flew in at nine last night to find him waiting for me.'

'I took her straight to the Pathology Department at St Bede's where they were holding the bodies.' Vaughan put in.

'It wasn't Max,' she said. 'It was as simple as that. I just knew, in spite of all those terrible injuries. Oh, he was the right colour and size, but it just wasn't him. Christ, I've never felt so relieved in my life.'

There were actually tears in her eyes. I patted that lovely face and said to Vaughan, 'You'll have to come up with something a little more concrete than that, surely?'

'We have,' he said. 'Or rather, Dr St Claire did. A question of the middle finger on the right hand.'

'Max put it into the cog wheels of an old-fashioned mangle when he was ten,' she said. 'The end was nipped off. It's the sort of thing that wouldn't be noticed. The end of the finger looks quite normal, there's even a nail, but when he puts his hands together you see that the middle finger of the right hand is a quarter of an inch less than the other. When I was a little girl he used to put his hands together to show me. It was a kind of joke between us.'

I nodded, trying hard to take it all in for I was already beginning to feel tired. The shock had been too great.

I said to Vaughan. 'All right, what's it all about?'

'Let's look at all possibilities,' he said. 'St Claire is an important man. Has direct responsibility for all Intelligence activities within the NATO alliance and a unique background in Far Eastern affairs, particularly Chinese. He's been heavily involved behind the scenes in the Paris peace talks over Vietnam.'

'And you think someone's snatched him?'

'I think it's the most likely explanation of what's happened. The only feasible one.' He took another photo from his briefcase and passed it across. 'Recognise him?'

It was Colonel Chen-Kuen, not a hair out of place and smiling faintly.

I said, 'I'll never forget him as long as I live. St Claire and I picked him out of several hundred photos the CIA showed us after our escape.'

'I was aware of that.' He put the photo back in its place. 'He's been head of Chinese Intelligence Section C, which is their Western European Sector, for about a year now operating out of Tirana in Albania.'

'And you think he's behind this business? You think he's got Max?'

'Perhaps.' He shrugged. 'At the moment we're struggling in the dark.

It was Sean O'Hara who made the obvious point. 'If they wanted to lay their hands on General St Claire, why not get on with it? Why all this tomfoolery concerning Ellis?'

'Look at it this way,' Vaughan said. 'If they'd simply kidnapped St Claire, everyone would have known it within hours. There would have been a world-wide stink. Questions in the U.N. The lot. But if they could make it seem that he was dead . . .'

'So the Ward woman was working for them?'

'She had to be.'

'And yet they killed her,' Helen said softly.

'The kind of people they are. Anything for the cause. I don't know who the substitute for your brother was. Probably some poor devil off the docks somewhere carefully selected beforehand.'

'And how would they get into the Foulness area?' Sean said. 'I've always had to produce a pass myself.'

Vaughan shrugged. 'Determined men could get ashore at the River Crouch end with very little trouble.'

I shook my head which was hurting even more by then. 'But they must have known they wouldn't stand much of a chance of getting away with a thing like that. Of the body passing muster.'

'Why not?' he said. 'General St Claire was seen to enter the area. Was checked through the Special Branch point and stated his destination as your cottage. With Sheila Ward's phone call to Dr O'Hara to damn you utterly, I'd say they had a fair chance that the body in question would be automatically accepted as that of the general.'

'And Sheila?'

'Probably thought she was to be a witness against you and the idea was that you were to be dead yourself, remember.'

The pain was terrible now. I turned blindly, pushing my head into Helen's shoulder and Sean said anxiously, 'What is it, Ellis?'

I told him and he went out quickly. Helen said, 'I'm going to stay in the village for a few days to be near you, Ellis. They didn't have a room vacant at the inn but the landlord has very kindly let me have the old Mill cottage by the bridge that he usually rents out during the summer.'

I think she was talking to keep me going. In any event Sean re-entered within a couple of minutes with a hypodermic and gave me an injection.

'That should help you sleep. As I said earlier, I'm afraid you'll be subject to various rather unpleasant symptoms for the next few days.'

I said to Vaughan, 'What about Max?'

'We'll be doing everything we can, but it's one hell of a difficult situation. We haven't a thing to go on. You'll still have to be held in official custody, but I'm hoping it won't be for long.'

I was going to argue, but I was too damn tired. Sean rang the bell on the desk and Flattery came in. 'Take Mr Jackson to his room and keep a close eye on him. I'll see him later this afternoon.'

Flattery took me by the arm and helped me outside. When we went up in the lift he put an arm about my shoulders.

'You lean on me, sir,' he said. 'You don't look too good.'

A change for the better indeed and I took full advantage of his offer, particularly when we got out of the lift and started across the narrow catwalk.

And then, half-way across, one of his feet became inextricably mixed in mine and his strong right arm was no longer in evidence as I went headlong, rolling towards the railing. I distinctly felt his foot planted squarely in the small of my back, helping me on my way to roll under the bottom rail and drop sixty feet to the flagstones below.

I grabbed at the rail, one leg already in space and then another voice echoed with mine and Thompson came running along the catwalk from the far end.

They got me on my feet between them, Flattery repeating several times that he simply couldn't understand how it had happened. A nasty accident narrowly averted, that seemed to be the general feeling.

But not to me. God knows what Sean had pumped into me for I was already half-asleep as they put me to bed, but still awake enough to remember the feel of that foot in the back, to notice the look in Flattery's eyes as he went out backwards, closing the door and locking it.

Flattery, for reasons best known to himself, had just tried to murder me. A hell of a thought to go to sleep on.

Caught between the shadow lines of sleep and wakening when strange things fill the mind, his face seemed to float up out of darkness, full of malevolence. I blinked a couple of times, murmuring disjointed words and when I opened my eyes again, he was still there, crouched over me. The expression had changed to one of apparent concern.

'Are you all right, Mr Jackson?'

I pushed myself up on one elbow. 'What time is it?'

'About seven o'clock, sir. You've slept like a log all day. Dr O'Hara would like to see you.'

I nodded slowly, my mind still dulled from whatever it was Sean had given me. 'All right, where is he?'

'Downstairs, sir. Shall I give you a hand?'

I shook my head wearily. 'No, I'll be all right, but I'd like a shower. I feel half-doped.'

'Dr O'Hara did say he was in something of a hurry, sir. I understand he wants to start back for London as soon as possible.'

I was still half-asleep and doped up to the eyeballs so that the memory of the incident on the catwalk earlier in the day had faded considerably, just another part of the mad pattern of my dreams like that look on his face as I awakened.

I had my back to him as I pulled on my dressing gown and turning rather quickly, caught him off guard, that expression of utter malevolence on his face again. I suppose it was that which saved me for in spite of his sudden, genial smile I was as wary as a cat as I moved out in the corridor.

'Where's Thompson?'

'Night off,' he said, pausing to close my door. 'Lucky devil. His second Saturday this month.'

'So you're in charge tonight?'

'That's it, sir.'

All this delivered in bluff, genial tones that put my teeth on edge because I didn't believe a word of it. I moved along the corridor towards the door to the catwalk, fighting to clear the greyness from my head.

Flattery said, 'Not that way tonight, sir, raining like hell it is.'

I paused at the lift doors. He reached over my shoulder and pressed one of the buttons. The doors slid open instantly only there was no lift, just a couple of steel cables rising out of a dark cavity.

It had all happened so quickly that it almost succeeded for I was completely off-balance. He gave me a shove in the back that sent me staggering forward. I grabbed for the steel cables, twisted round in a circle and gave him both feet in the chest as he leaned in through the entrance.

It was hardly a crippling blow, for most of the energy in the thrust of my body was expended in getting me back to safety, but it certainly sent him staggering back into the opposite wall. I made it to firm ground and ran a yard or two along the corridor, turning to face him.

'Who put you up to it, Flattery?'

He stood up slowly, wiping blood from his mouth, madness in his eyes. 'Bloody little squirt,' he said. 'I'll show you. No one to help you up here. Dr O'Hara just left after phoning through to see how you were. I told him you were all tucked up for the night.'

He moved fast for such a big man, the boxer in him coming out. He swung a tremendous right that would have broken my jaw if it had landed. I swerved slightly allowing him to plunge past me and slashed him across the kidneys with the edge of my hand. He went flat on his face with a cry, got up almost at once and lurched forwards, hands reaching to destroy, all his science forgotten.

I grabbed for his right wrist with both hands, twisting it round and up. I gave it an extra twist to dislocate the shoulder then ran him headfirst into the wall.

He was moaning with pain, blood on his face

and I dropped to one knee. 'I've asked you a question.'

He had plenty of animal courage, I'll give him that and told me where to go in pretty fair Anglo-Saxon.

'All right,' I said. 'So you're a hard man.'

I got him by the scruff of the neck, dragged him across to the lift and positioned him with his head over the edge. Then I stood up, a foot in his back to hold him steady and put my finger on the button.

'You'll be able to see it coming.' I said. 'A lovely way to go.'

I pressed the button and the cables moved. It was all it took. He broke wide open with a cry of fear, struggling furiously under my foot. I took my finger off the button and dropped to one knee beside him. He tried to move back, but I held him fast, his head still on the block.

'Now start talking.'

'I met this bloke in the village pub last night. Fruity as hell. Bow tie, shaven head, that sort of thing. Said his name was Dallywater.'

'So what happened?'

'He was doing all the buying. One double

after another. At first I thought he was just some old queer on the make, then he started talking about you.'

'And turned out to have friends who would find it convenient if I met with an accident?'

He nodded. 'That's it, but it took him four hours to get around to it. We ended up in his room.'

'How much?'

He coughed and spat blood into the darkness of the shaft. 'A thousand quid. A hundred down – the rest to come afterwards. He gave me the first instalment there and then. I couldn't believe it.'

'You bloody fool,' I said. 'You'd have got paid off all right, but not with any nine hundred pounds. Who was behind this?'

Not that I expected an answer to that one and he shook his head. 'All I know is, his name isn't Dallywater. It's Pendlebury.'

'How do you know that?'

'I had a look inside his car afterwards. He'd left one of the quarter lights open. There were some visiting cards in the glove compartment. I've got one with me. Right-hand ticket pocket.

And there was a book written under the same name with his picture on the back.'

'What kind of book?'

'Something to do with the east. Buddhism and that sort of stuff. *The Great Mystery,* that was it.'

I found the visiting card. *Rafe Pendlebury, Sargon House, Sidbury.* Sidbury, as I remembered, was somewhere near the Mendip Hills.

I gave the button another brief jab and Flattery cried out. 'I've told you the truth, I swear it, only he isn't there now. Told me he was leaving this morning. That he'd be in touch.'

I hoisted him to his feet and propped him against the wall. He stayed there, blood oozing from the smashed mouth and nose, his right arm held at an awkward angle. I suppose what happened then was the catalyst for everything that followed for until that moment I intended to take him to whoever was in charge of the place, insist that they contacted O'Hara and Hilary Vaughan as quickly as possible.

As I turned to press the button to bring the lift up, he came to life and lunged forward, his one good arm aimed for my back again, a repeat of his earlier performance. I pivoted sideways, he brushed against me and went headlong into the shaft without a cry.

When I brought the lift up, he was sprawled on top, his head twisted to one side in a way which could only mean his neck was broken. He was dead all right – no escaping that or the fact that it was going to look as if I'd killed him.

Getting out of there seemed in that single moment in time the most sensible thing I could do. I brought the lift up level with the opening and locked it back on to the automatic system which meant that he would ride up and down on top, hidden from view, until some maintenance man or other decided to check the shaft. From now on, I had to play it wholly by ear and needed more than a little luck, but then it was time for some of that. Things had certainly been running the other way for long enough. I got into the lift and took it down to the first floor.

When the doors opened, I peered out into a deserted corridor. Somewhere a radio played faintly and rain drummed against the window to the left. I stepped out and the lift doors closed behind me quietly.

I turned and saw the indicator light move down to the ground floor. It paused fractionally, then started to rise again. I turned, noticed a door opposite marked *Bathroom* and was inside in a moment.

I stood in darkness, the door open a crack and watched as the lift indicator came to rest and the doors opened. A couple of male nurses emerged, one of them a West Indian.

They moved along the corridor together and I heard the West Indian say, 'Not me, man. On a night like this I stay close to home. How about a game of cards later?'

The other man seemed to agree and moved off down the corridor and the West Indian opened the door of what was obviously his room and went in.

It occurred to me then that the bathroom was perhaps not the safest of places in which to avoid detection. I noticed a door marked *Linen* on the other side of the lift and moved across. Inside, it was not much more than a closet with white wooden shelves loaded with blankets and sheets.

The move had certainly been a judicious one

for as I peered out through the crack of the door, the West Indian emerged from his room in a bathrobe, a towel over one arm, a plastic toilet bag swinging from his other hand. He was whistling cheerfully, went into the bathroom and closed the door. The inside bolt moved into place with a definite click and the taps were turned on.

I didn't hesitate. I was out of the linen closet in a second, half-a-dozen quick strides took me to his door and I stepped inside.

It was larger than I had expected and extremely well furnished with a fitted carpet and Scandinavian bedroom suite. There was even a portable television on a table at the foot of the bed.

The wardrobe was well stocked with clothes. I helped myself to some corduroy slacks and a pair of suede chukka boots with elastic sides which looked as if they'd stay on in spite of being a size too large. There were three or four sweaters on the shelves and I simply grabbed the first one that came to hand, a heavy Norwegian job, and a pair of socks.

There was an overcoat behind the door, I was going to take it, then discovered an old faded

Burberry trenchcoat underneath. A much better proposition altogether. A cautious check on the corridor and I was back inside the linen closet.

I kept my pyjamas on – simply pulled the pants and sweater over them. The chukka boots were too large as I had surmised, but not uncomfortably so, and the Burberry I buttoned to the neck and turned up the collar.

There was an inevitability to it all now. It was as if the whole thing was already marked out and I was trapped by events, borne along inexorably towards a destination as yet unknown to me. I knew that, quite suddenly, with complete certainty and it gave me a strange feeling of confidence when I stepped into the corridor and opened the lift doors.

The basement seemed the safest place to go. The last place for anyone to be at half-past eight on a Saturday night whereas there was certain to be staff around at the ground floor level.

When the doors opened, I pressed the second floor button and quickly stepped out into the passage. The doors closed behind me and as the lift ascended, I moved forward between white painted walls.

At the far end, I found two or three steps leading to a stout wooden door, rain seeping through. It was bolted top and bottom. I eased them free, opened the door and found myself in a small dark area, steps leading up to the courtyard above.

I went up the steps without hesitation, hands in pockets, for it seemed to me that to look in any way out of the ordinary would be the worst possible thing.

But I was as yet only half free as I walked briskly across the courtyard and went along the side of the main block. I didn't fancy my chances with that electrified fence which only left the main gate and that meant transport.

I took my one chance, running across the lawn at the front of the house towards the beech trees, those same trees I had seen earlier that day from behind bars and made it in what seemed like record time considering my condition.

Now here is a strange thing. At that time and for some time afterwards, I felt better than I had at any stage since the game began, gripped by a fierce exhilaration that reminded me strongly of that moment on the other side of the river from Tay Son with St Claire at the start of our incredible journey. It certainly provided me with the fuel for what was to follow.

I moved through the trees and positioned myself in the bushes at a point where I noticed that the road down from the main block turned at right angles for the final run to the gate. It seemed reasonable to suppose that any vehicle coming that way would have to slow right down.

Within five minutes, a private car appeared, to be followed by another very quickly. Neither of them was suitable for my purposes. I waited hopefully for another quarter of an hour, getting wetter and wetter, wondering whether I might stand there all night when suddenly there was the roaring of a much larger engine and an old three-ton Bedford truck rolled out of the night. It stopped altogether, then moved forward slowly as the driver negotiated the bend.

When I clambered over the tailgate, I saw in the light of the lamps at the edge of the drive that the thing was empty except for a couple of small packing cases. Which left me only one place to go and as the truck increased speed, I stood on the tailgate, hauled myself up on top of the canvas tilt and lay face down and prayed.

I suppose it was the rain which helped more than anything for by now it was hammering down with real force. When we reached the gates, the truck braked to a halt, but left the engine ticking over.

I closed my eyes tight and tried to make myself even smaller as feet clattered down the steps of the single-storeyed guard house. They moved to the rear of the truck, paused as someone peered over the tailgate and then a voice called something unintelligible. The gates creaked open and we moved out into the road.

I gave it a couple of minutes, then raised my head and saw to my horror that we were already approaching the outskirts of the village. I crawled backwards, scrambled down on to the tailgate and got ready to jump as the truck slowed to negotiate a narrow bridge. A moment later, I was rolling over twice on wet grass at the side of the road.

I sat up, for some reason choking back laughter and the truck faded into the night. But there was another sound, a steady, rather monotonous creaking, a regular heavy splashing. I moved to the parapet of the bridge, looked across and saw an old mill water wheel turning in the fast-flowing stream.

The old Mill cottage by the bridge, wasn't that what Helen said? I found it on the other side, a white painted fence with *Mill House* on a board on the gate and the cottage itself beyond, Elizabethan from the look of it, with a thatched roof.

I moved round to the side and found that Alfa parked there, glistening in the rain in the light of a lamp above the door. I peered through the window into a surprisingly modern kitchen and saw Helen standing at the stove, stirring a pan.

That flair for drama of mine coming to the surface again, I simply opened the door and stepped inside. She whirled round, a frown on her face, then stood there, staring at me in utter amazement.

'Ellis!'

'In the flesh,' I said.

She crossed to me with a kind of rush, flung her arms around my neck and kissed me – and with real passion. One hell of an improvement on Paris.

I said, 'You'll get wet. I'm soaking.'

'That's obvious. She started to unbutton my Burberry. 'Dr O'Hara left here for London not ten minutes ago. According to him, you were nicely tucked up for the night. Now what's going on?'

She stood there clutching the wet Burberry looking more beautiful than any woman had a right to do and clever with it – two doctorates and another on the way. So I decided on the direct approach.

'I've killed a man,' I said simply. 'Or at least that's the way it's going to look when they find him.'

When I finally finished, we were sitting facing each other on the opposite sides of the table. She believed me, there was no doubt about that, but her distress was plain.

'But why, Ellis? What could be the motive?'

'All right,' I said. 'Accepting Vaughan's version of things, an important part of the original plan was quite simply that I should appear to be a raving lunatic under the influence of dangerous drugs who then committed suicide. Fortunately for me, I vomited most of the poison and Sean arrived in time to do exactly the right thing.'

'I know that,' she said. 'Go on.'

'Now the fact that I'm alive, no matter how guilty I look, is more than inconvenient because it means there's always a chance that if I keep on yelling loudly enough, someone might take a little notice.'

'Not take things quite so much for granted, you mean?'

'Exactly. Much better if poor, raving Ellis Jackson throws himself off the catwalk or jumps down the lift shaft. If either of those things had happened it would have been accepted as a second, only this time successful, attempt at suicide.'

'But not by Vaughan, surely?'

'Dead right, only they don't know how far

their little scheme's come unstuck already, do they?'

She shook her head slowly. 'Even so, this Flattery business is terrible. You should have stayed, Ellis. Now things look blacker than ever.'

'Oh, no they don't.' I produced the visiting card. 'Not as long as I've got this. The mysterious Mr Pendlebury's got some explaining to do. There'll be an R.A.C. handbook in the Alfa. Give me the keys.'

'What do you want that for?'

'To find out exactly where Sidbury is.'

'You don't mean to say you intend to go chasing off after this wretched man yourself.'

'Have you any objections?'

She appeared to hesitate, then sighed heavily, reached for her handbag and took out the keys which she threw across the table.

'For such a clever man you can sometimes be incredibly stupid, Ellis, but have it your own way.'

I went out into the rain, unlocked the Alfa and got into the driving seat. I found the R.A.C. handbook and looked up Sidbury in the gazetteer. It was there all right. Population one hundred and twenty. One pub, one garage and not much else, on the edge of the Mendip Hills not far from Wells. I had a look at the map then returned to the cottage.

Helen was not in the kitchen. I opened the far door and found myself in a pleasant, oak-beamed lounge. There was a stone hearth large enough to roast an ox and a log fire burned brightly. She was sitting beside it, her hand on the telephone.

'Who are you thinking of calling – Vaughan?'

'I can't,' she said. 'He phoned earlier to say he'd been called to Paris for a NATO Intelligence conference to discuss this whole affair.'

'When does he get back?'

'Sometime tomorrow morning. He's flying in on the RAF Support Command mail plane first thing.'

'All right, that rules him out for the moment which only leaves Sean and he'll still be en route for London.'

'I could always phone the police.'

'You could at that, but the way things look at the moment, I suspect they'd be more inclined to clap me in irons than anything else.'

'True enough,' she said. 'I suppose the next thing you'll tell me is that you can't afford to lose precious time. That it's all for Max.'

I was surprised, not really understanding what she was driving at. 'What else?'

'Oh, no, Ellis, not that. Not the lie in the soul at this stage in the game. You want to do this for Ellis Jackson and nobody else. They put the boot into you, whoever they are – isn't that the phrase? Now you want to put it into them, only harder. Your primary response to almost every situation is a violent one.'

'Thank you, Dr Kildare,' I told her, but there was a certain truth in what she said. Enough to make me feel uneasy. It was as if one had looked into the mirror and had no liking for what was there.

She said coolly, 'This place Sidbury – where is it?'

'Edge of the Mendips near Wells.'

'I don't know that part of the country.'

'Seventy miles or so from here. An hour and a half in the Alfa.'

'All right,' she said. 'On one condition.'

'What's that?'

'That I drive. Your reflexes aren't up to it, not in the state you're in.'

I could have argued about that, but it wouldn't have done any good and in any case, as I turned and went back into the kitchen, there was another of those clicks inside my head and the light shade mushroomed above my head.

'Wait for me in the car,' she said. 'I won't be long.'

We were back in that echo chamber again and as the walls started to undulate, I went out into the rain, got into the front passenger seat and strapped myself in.

I closed my eyes, breathed slowly and regularly and tried to remember everything Black Max had ever taught me about relaxation because nothing was going to stop me now. I was going to get to Sidbury and squeeze the truth of things out of friend Pendlebury if it was the last thing I did.

The temple of truth

6

I had expected her to say something about St Claire, to make some kind of comment on the situation, but she didn't. Perhaps that was the true reason she had insisted on driving – to occupy herself fully and crowd thought out, for brother-sister relationships when they are close, are confused affairs at best, strange currents pulling every which-way just beneath the surface.

She worshipped St Claire, always had, which was understandable enough. She was a different person when he was around, smiling slightly anxiously, always to hand with anything from an ashtray to a Bloody Mary at the snap of his fingers.

It wasn't the kind of night for much traffic, heavy relentless rain clearing the road from

Newbury on. Some of the most beautiful country in England all around and it might as well not have existed for all we could see of it.

She drove with all the fierce, dedicated concentration of the professional Grand Prix driver, using the gears constantly, she and that magnificent car against the darkness and the torrential rain.

None of which left much time for conversation which suited me admirably. By the time we reached Marlborough, I was feeling reasonably myself again or at least, confident of retaining some sort of control. We moved on through Chippenham, dropping down into Bath in just on the hour.

About a mile out of Bath on the A39 as we were passing through Corston, she pulled in to the kerb at a public telephone box without warning and switched off the engine.

'I'm going to phone Sean O'Hara. He should be home by now.'

She was out of the Alfa before I could reply, taking the keys with her, probably because of some basic fear that I might run out on her. Not that I hadn't thought of it, but circumstances were against me. I helped myself to a cigarette from her handbag, got out and half-opened the booth door so that I could hear what was going on.

She was talking fast and looking frustrated. 'But surely you have another number at which he can be reached?'

From the look on her face, she obviously wasn't getting anywhere so I reached in and took the receiver from her hand. 'Who's speaking?'

The voice was solid like a rock, but perfectly polite. 'The porter at Carley Mansions. Dr O'Hara has an apartment here, sir.'

'Has he been in this evening?'

'About half-an-hour ago, sir, and left again within ten minutes. All his professional calls tonight are being handled by Dr Meyer Goldberg at Sloane 8235.'

'This is a private call.'

'Then I'm sorry, but I can't help you, sir. Dr O'Hara didn't say where he could be reached. Never does on his night off, sir.'

'Wise man,' I said. 'When he does come in, tell him Ellis Jackson phoned and will phone again, probably in the morning. It's most urgent.'

I replaced the receiver and eased Helen out into the rain. 'If I know my Sean he'll be hard at it in some other bed than his own till the small hours. He has one great weakness – anything female between the ages of eighteen and twenty-five. He should consult an analyst.'

She actually managed to laugh. 'Ellis Jackson, you're a complete and unmitigated bastard.'

'Now don't go all clinical on me,' I told her. 'We want to be on the other side of Chewton Mendip which is a good ten miles from here so let's get going.'

We moved on through the quiet hills, reaching Sidbury just after ten, a couple of narrow streets flanked by fifteenth century houses, deserted in the heavy rain. We slowed as an inn loomed out of the shadows on our left, a dozen or so cars parked outside and then I noticed a garage on the corner opposite and the lights were still on above the pumps.

'Try there.' I said and she nodded and pulled over.

A middle-aged man in an old raincoat and

tweed cap was standing in a small glass booth at the entrance, coins and notes stacked on the shelf before him in neat piles. He looked up in some surprise when Helen touched the horn, but came out at once. She asked for eight gallons and I got out and moved round to stand at his side.

'A dirty night.'

'That it is,' he said. 'I was just closing.'

'I'm looking for a place called Sargon House,' I said. 'Owned by a chap called Pendlebury.'

He seemed surprised. 'Come far, have you?'

'London,' I said. 'Why?'

He put the filler cap back on. 'Long way for nothing. They usually finish up there around ten o'clock.'

'Finish what?' I asked him.

'Why, the services. That's what you've come for, ain't it? That's what they all come for.'

It was Helen who cut in smoothly, producing a five pound note from her bag and holding it out to him through the window. 'I know, it's very annoying. We broke down in Newbury, then I took a wrong turning on the way out of Bath and we ended up miles out of the way.'

He glanced down, really noticing her for the

first time and his expression changed as most men's did when confronted with that extraordinary face.

'Can't read the signs properly on a night like this,' he said as if wishing to assure her that it wasn't her fault.

He went into the booth and I got back into the Alfa. 'Quick thinking.'

She didn't get a chance to reply for he was already back with the change. 'Straight on to the edge of the village, over the bridge and sharp right. Keep on that road through the woods for another quarter of a mile. You can't miss it. He has a board by the gate listing all the service times, just like church.'

He didn't sound as if he approved but she thanked him and drove away.

'All very mysterious,' she said as we went over the bridge. 'What do you think our Mr Pendlebury's up to?'

'God knows,' I said. 'We'll just have to wait and see.'

We moved on along a dark tunnel through trees beside a high stone wall, towards a patch of light on the left that finally blossomed into a couple of lamps suspended from a wrought iron frame above high gates which stood wide.

There was a board beside the gate handsomely painted in gold and blue. It carried the legend *Temple of Truth* and listed various activities underneath, including week-long retreats and the times of services. Saturday night was eight till ten. Pendlebury's name appeared at the bottom of the list, naked and unadorned.

'Well, at least he hasn't called himself bishop,' I said. 'Let's get on up to the house and see what it's all about.'

The drive moved on through pine trees emptying into about a couple of acres of terraced gardens containing the house. It was Georgian and not all that large. A couple of dozen cars were parked in the gravelled circle in front of the entrance and most of them seemed to be in the Jaguar-Bentley bracket.

Helen pulled in at the end of the line and I got out and moved towards the porch. The front door stood open and I paused by the steps and waited for her to join me.

'It looks as if they're still at it,' she said. 'What do we do now?'

'Assume a suitably devout expression and join the party.'

As I paused in the porch, she put a hand on my arm. 'I'm not so sure this is a good idea.'

I said, 'You want Max back, don't you?'

I didn't give her a chance to discuss it any further and went through into the wide hall beyond. It was illuminated by candlelight, half-a-dozen of them burning in a many-branched silver holder standing on a small table and there was the heavy, all-pervading scent of incense everywhere.

There was a murmur of voices from a large double door to one side by the stairs. It was slightly ajar and I pushed it open a little so that we could look inside.

The room was long and rather narrow, curtains drawn across the windows at one side, Chinese tapestries covering the wall on the other. Thirty or forty people sat crosslegged on the floor in the half-darkness for, like the hall, the only illumination came from candles, in this case positioned in front of a kind of altar on which stood a gold-painted figure of Buddha.

There was the usual small fire burning in a

bowl before it and a man prayed there, stretched out on the floor like a penitent, arms out on either side in the shape of a cross. He was wearing a saffron robe which left one shoulder bare and his head was shaved.

When he stood up and turned, I saw that he was a European with a rather fine face and calm, wise eyes.

'Pendlebury?' Helen breathed in my ear.

I don't know why, but I was inclined to think it was, purely on hunch.

His voice when he spoke was as calm as the eyes and melodious in the extreme. I think it was that which struck the first really jarring note for it occurred to me suddenly that it was as if he were not a truly real person, but someone playing a part.

He said, 'And so I give you a text on which to meditate, sisters and brothers all. To do good – this is too easy. To be good – this is all there is. This is the golden key.'

He blessed them, hand high, then moved off to one side. It was only after he had gone that his audience started to rise.

It was then that I noticed the monks – two

of them. Saffron robes, shaven heads just like Pendlebury – only these were Chinese. The most surprising thing was the collecting bags. They carried one each and as the audience started to file out, people paused to make their contributions. No silver collection this. Only the rustle of paper money. I stepped back, taking Helen by the arm and moved into the shadows by the stairs.

'What now?' she demanded.

'We'll see if his holiness will grant us an audience. Give me a couple of fivers and leave me to do the talking.'

As she got the money out of her bag the audience started to emerge, mainly women from what I could see. Affluent, middle-aged and anxious. The kind who, having everything, end up by finding they have nothing and search ceaselessly for some means of filling the vacuum.

They moved out through the front door shepherded by the two monks, one of whom moved off almost immediately. As the other eased the last couple of visitors out and closed the door, I stepped from the shadows by the stairs and stood waiting, Helen at my shoulder.

When he turned and found us there his actions were extremely interesting. His right foot eased forward, his body dropping into the basic defence pose common to all the martial arts. Nothing too obvious to the uninitiated, but it was there.

I said brightly. 'We were wondering if Mr Pendlebury could possibly spare us a few minutes.'

He relaxed completely and actually managed a smile of sorts. 'The *guru* is always extremely tired after a service,' he said in excellent English. 'You must understand this. The mental strain is so intense. He is always available to help those in need or genuine seekers after self-knowledge, but by arrangement in advance.'

I produced the two five pound notes Helen had given me and offered them to him. 'I didn't get a chance to contribute earlier. The service was an inspiration.'

'Wasn't it?' he said simply, taking the two notes and stuffing them into the already bulging collection bag which he held in his left hand. 'I will see if the *guru* will see you.'

He opened a door to the left of the stairs

and moved inside. Helen said quietly. 'I didn't like him.'

'Any particular reason?'

'It was the eyes. They didn't smile when his mouth did. A funny kind of monk.'

'Not really.' I said softly. '*Judo*, *karate* – all the martial arts are just a Japanese development of the ancient Chinese art of Shaolin Temple Boxing which first came from India with Zen Buddhism in the sixth century and was improved on by the monks of Shaolin Temple in Honan Province.'

'That sounds like a pretty wild sort of scene for priests.'

'They were hard times,' I said. 'You didn't get far by turning the other cheek.'

The door opened, the monk emerged and stood to one side, motioning us in. 'The *guru* can spare you five minutes, but he is very tired. It would be appreciated if you do not stay beyond the stated time. Any further meeting will have to be by appointment.'

I moved inside, Helen behind me a little reluctantly and I looked around quickly. The room was large, the wall draped with superb Chinese tapestries, collector's items without a doubt and the floor was covered with hand-woven silken rugs of equal magnificence.

Pendlebury was on his knees in front of a small figurine of Buddha set in a small alcove and the monk whispered in my ear, 'He will not keep you long.' He went out closing the door softly behind him.

There was a log fire in a wrought iron basket on the hearth, a very English touch, but the ebony desk was Chinese as were the ceramics on the shelves in the large alcove beside the fireplace. Several figurines, a selection of bowls and four or five quite exquisite vases. I moved across casually to examine them.

The golden voice said, 'I see you are admiring my little collection.'

He was older than I had at first thought, the skin pouched beneath the eyes and tight over the cheekbones. In the candlelight out there he had looked good. Somehow ageless, but I realised now that he was just an old pro, at his best on stage and looking about a hundred years old off.

There was a kind of warmth there when he

reached out to touch one of the figurines, a woman on horseback in wimple and conical hat.

'An example of Ming Dynasty work at its best.'

Helen said, 'These things must be worth a great deal of money.'

'How can one put a price on beauty?' At that he was back playing a part again moving to the desk and seating himself. 'In what way can I serve you? You need guidance, perhaps?'

'You could put it like that.' I took Helen by the elbow and led her to the chair on the opposite side of the desk. 'My name's Ellis Jackson. Does that mean anything to you?'

It had roughly the same effect as a good, solid kick between the legs. He suddenly looked older than it was humanly possible to be, a walking corpse, the skin of his face drying before my eyes.

He tried hard and failed miserably. 'I – I'm afraid not.'

'Now that I really do find surprising,' I told him. 'When we consider the fact that only last night, you offered someone a thousand pounds to see me dead.'

But by now, he'd managed to regain some kind of control. 'I'm afraid I don't know what you're talking about. Here, we are concerned only with the conquest of self. How could we reconcile this with attempts to bring about the destruction of a fellow human being?'

'You can keep that stuff for the paying customers,' I said. 'But my friend here has a problem you might be able to help us with. She's lost her brother and for some odd reason I've got complete faith in your ability to tell us where he is.'

Pendlebury looked uncertainly at Helen. 'Your brother? I'm afraid I don't quite understand.'

'Brigadier-General James Maxwell St Claire,' I put in.

He started to his feet and at the same moment an arm slid across my throat. I suppose he must have been standing behind one of the tapestries or – more probably – there was a concealed door.

In any event, I put my heel down hard enough into the bare instep to crack bone and brought both elbows backwards, striking beneath the ribs on either side. But he was good – damn good. He hung on with everything he had because that's what he'd dedicated his whole life to learning to do, but his arm slackened. Not much, but enough for me to get my fingers to his wrists. I tore them free, dropped to one knee and threw him across the room. He knocked Pendlebury out of his chair into those shelves in the alcove and several thousand pounds' worth of rare pottery was scattered across the floor. Some of the pieces actually bounced and others simply disintegrated.

Pendlebury was on his knees, howling in anguish like a hurt dog, but I had other things to think about because just then, the other monk burst in through the door.

They're all the same, most of the really expert exponents of the martial arts. They think technique all the time. They spend about twenty years of their life mastering *karate* or *judo* or *aikido* and in the end, their own excellence is against them because they operate best when they get the same standard in return from their opponents.

This one gave the usual terrible cry to frighten me and struck a typical *karate* stance, assuming he'd get it back. So I dropped in a prizefighter's crouch, just to confuse him. He hesitated and was lost because as I led with the right, I switched techniques and pulled the rug out from under him.

In other circumstances it might have seemed amusing, but I was beginning to lose my sense of humour fast. As he started to get up, I gave him a boot in the face, real old English back alley variety and he went against the wall hard, slid to the floor and didn't get up.

As I turned, Helen cried a warning. The black Red Dragon tapesty on the rear wall ballooned out like a sail in the wind and three more Chinese burst through, conventionally attired in neat, dark suits, but yelling loud enough to blow the place apart. There wasn't much I could do, particularly as someone tripped me neatly from the rear around then, sending me headlong amongst those flying feet.

I was on my face trying to crawl, head singing and then the walls started to undulate again and I closed my eyes hard and tried to stop myself from drifting off. My arms were behind my back now and Helen screamed again and there was a voice calling my name insistently.

'Ellis – Ellis. Look at me.'

A hand slapped my face gently so I opened my eyes and looked straight into the pleasant concerned face of Colonel Chen-Kuen.

Down among the dead men

7

Another aspect of that privileged nightmare I had been living, but this time I was conscious of a kind of relief for now, beyond any possibility of doubt, I knew that I had been right from the beginning. That things had truly been as I had imagined. This man was no figment of some disordered mind. This man was flesh and blood.

I lay there, half-conscious, my face against the floor as someone held my hands behind my back and I listened to him as he spoke briefly to the others in Chinese.

There was no sign of Helen, she had presumably already been moved, and I watched as Pendlebury's two assistants were helped out of the room, both of them looking decidedly the worse for wear.

Pendlebury sat huddled in the chair behind

his desk, head in hands, occasionally looking up to stare hopelessly around the room, an expression of utter despair on his face, completely unable to cope with things as they had developed.

Chen-Kuen went to the desk and leaned across, one hand on his shoulder, talking earnestly in a low voice. Whatever he was saying, Pendlebury didn't like for he shook his head helplessly from side-to-side.

Chen-Kuen raised his voice, as if to impress the seriousness of things on him and said firmly in English, 'But my dear Pendlebury, it must be done. I'll leave Pai-Chang to handle it. All you have to do is give him whatever assistance he requires. You can both follow later.'

Pendlebury nodded, stood up and went out in a kind of daze. Chen-Kuen watched him go, frowning slightly. He helped himself to a cigarette from a box on the desk and one of the Chinese, a small, vital looking man in a well-tailored suit of dark worsted, offered him a light. This was presumably the Pai-Chang referred to and they spoke together briefly in Chinese.

'We must leave at once,' Chen-Kuen said. 'I'm already considerably later than I had intended. I leave things here in your hands with every confidence. You know what to do. I shall look for you tomorrow.'

'And the old man?' Pai-Chang said. 'Shall I bring him with me or does he carry on here?'

Chen-Kuen shook his head. 'This place is of no further use to us. As for Pendlebury . . .' He sighed and looked as if he genuinely meant it. 'A broken man. He has lost his faith and that is always dangerous.'

'The same way as the other?' Pai-Chang asked.

'I think it would be the sensible thing.'

We were alone now, the three of us and I made some sort of movement which immediately caught his eye. He nodded to Pai-Chang who crossed the room quickly and heaved me to my feet with no apparent effort.

'My dear Ellis, you must sit down,' Chen-Kuen said. 'You don't look at all well.'

Pai-Chang shoved me into a chair and Chen-Kuen sat on the edge of the desk. 'Still the same old Ellis – as violent and unpredictable as ever.

How many dead men did you leave behind at Marsworth Hall?'

'Only one,' I said. 'The bastard your friend Pendlebury bribed to see me off. Surely you could have done better than him? He's a joke. Nobody could believe in him for more than five minutes together at any one time.'

He sighed. 'One must use the tools which come to hand in my kind of work, Ellis, and Pendlebury had his uses. I wouldn't underestimate him, by the way. Hundreds of people, those who have visited him here, think of him as a new Messiah.'

I let that one go. 'What have you done with St Claire?'

He didn't attempt to prevaricate although I suppose there wouldn't have been much point. He simply said, 'All right, Ellis, cards on the table. Just tell me how things stand.'

'Gladly,' I said. 'You've had it. The right people know all about you, thank God. You're on borrowed time.'

He didn't seem in the least put out, stood up and walked out quickly leaving Pai-Chang in charge. I tried to ease my wrists without much success for they had been tied very securely with a rather thin cord which bit into the flesh painfully. Pai-Chang came across at the first sign of movement and examined them.

He moved back to the desk satisfied and helped himself to a cigarette, leaving me to my own dark thoughts. God knows, but it was a mess whichever way you looked at it.

A moment later Chen-Kuen returned, walking briskly across to the desk and sitting on the edge again. He smiled amicably. 'All is revealed, Ellis, as they used to say in those old melodramas.'

'What are you driving at?'

'I now know exactly what the situation is. Very simple really. I had a quiet word with Dr St Claire. Explained how unpleasant the consequences would be for you if she didn't tell me the truth.' He shook his head. 'You two are the only ones who know about Pendlebury and this place, Ellis. You weren't being very honest with me.'

He sounded exactly like some fatherly headmaster reproving a recalcitrant schoolboy. I could have called him a name or two, but there didn't seem any point.

'What happens now?'

'The girl can leave with me. A nice surprise for her brother. But you, Ellis.' He gave another of those sighs of his. 'This time we really must finish what was started.'

'It was a rotten idea from the first,' I said. 'You never stood more than a fifty-fifty chance of getting away with it.'

'But still worth it,' he said. 'So much neater to have St Claire officially dead and beneath the sod, as the Irish say. Things were rushed, that was the trouble. Certain pressures built up and we were forced to move a little too quickly for comfort, but that, as they say, is another story and of little interest to you now.'

'Just tell me one thing. Who was the substitute you provided?'

'I believe he was bosun on a Panamanian timber boat. Brought in from Antwerp as an illegal immigrant. He will not be missed because he was never here.'

'And Sheila Ward?' It hurt to ask that one.

'Had worked for us for four years.'

'And you killed her.'

'She was what you would term expendable or

if you would prefer it another way, more use to us dead than alive.'

'You bastard,' I said. 'And what good has it done you at the end of things? Your bloody plan didn't work.'

'But I still have General St Claire which is all that counts,' he said. 'War is war. Your side and mine are engaged in one whether you like to admit it or not; in war, people die and how they die is immaterial. It is all one in the end. We will win and you will lose because history is on our side.'

Strange, but those words were words I'd heard before from Madame Ny. The same sentiments, the same phrases, the same absolutely implacable belief in the rightness of the cause.

He stood up, stubbed out his cigarette and said rather formally, 'And now I must leave you and with a certain regret. We might have been friends you and I in other circumstances, but there it is.'

He walked out quickly and Pai-Chang went with him. I sat there in the chair, straining hopelessly at my wrists and a moment later, Pendlebury came in. He was wearing slacks and a polo neck sweater and when he reached into the box for a cigarette, his hand was shaking.

'You shouldn't have come here,' he said. 'It was a stupid thing to do.'

'What are they going to do with me?'

He managed to light the cigarette with some difficulty and stood looking at me, a kind of helpless horror on his face.

'Oh, for God's sake, man,' I said. 'Pull yourself together and tell me the worst.'

'All right,' he said. 'There's an ornamental lake on the other side of the trees from the house, sixty feet deep at one end where the old quarry used to be.'

'Don't tell me any more,' I said. 'Let me guess. You and Pai-Chang take me out in some convenient boat and put me over the side with fifty pounds of chain round my ankles.' I laughed in his face. 'You poor bloody booby. When I go, you go. I heard Chen-Kuen give the order.'

His face turned very pale. 'It's a lie.'

'Have it your own way.' I shrugged. 'I'd say it was the logical thing to do. You know too much.'

He said slowly, 'I won't believe it. It can't be

true.' And then as the thought struck him, a new light came into his eyes. 'You *are* lying. I know you are. If they spoke together at all, they'd have spoken in Chinese. They always do.'

'One of the few useful accomplishments I picked up in North Vietnam,' I said in Cantonese. 'Or hadn't you heard?'

He stared at me in horror, mouth gaping, but was unable to take things further for at that moment, Pai-Chang returned. He heaved me from the chair and pushed me ahead of him into the hall. We went along a narrow passage towards the rear of the building, opened one of several doors and he shoved me inside. I caught a brief glimpse of a small, narrow storeroom and then the door closed leaving me in total darkness. I waited a couples of minutes for my eyes to get adjusted and then started a cautious reconnaissance, following the wall, one foot extended. The cupboard was quite bare so I slid down to the ground and started to strain at my bonds.

It was perhaps an hour later when the door was flung open and Pai-Chang appeared. He was wearing a navy blue anorak and looked tough and very competent as he pulled me out into the corridor and shoved me along in front of him.

Pendlebury was waiting for us in the entrance hall. He was obviously under considerable strain and looked faintly ridiculous in an old oilskin coat a size too large for him.

He glanced at me nervously, then dropped his gaze as Pai-Chang pushed me out of the front door and down the steps into the rain. Pendlebury stumbled along behind and the Chinese waited for him, face impassive before starting across the lawn.

The rain fell without pause, there was the heavy rank smell of rotting vegetation as we neared the lake and then the dark shape of an old boathouse loomed out of the night. Pai-Chang unbolted the heavy wooden doors and pulled one of them open. He moved inside ahead of us, there was a click and a light came on over the door.

The boathouse ran out into the lake itself and a narrow wooden jetty extended even further, a single light burning at the far end, presumably turned on by the same switch as the other.

There were several old rowing skiffs on view plus the accumulated junk of years, but Pai-Chang took me by the arm and pushed me along the jetty towards the light.

A boat was moored there, a medium size rowing boat with oars inside, half-full of water as far as I could judge. The rain bounced from the wet planking and our feet made a hollow booming sound.

Pai-Chang pushed me down on a pile of old, rotting canvas and said to Pendlebury, 'Watch him. I'll get the boat.'

As he moved away I said to Pendlebury in a low voice, 'You'll never get by on your own, can't you see that? I'm the only person who can help you now.'

In the sickly, yellow light of the lamp he looked terrible. As if he might die of fright at any moment and his hands were shaking again.

'What am I going to do?' he whispered in a hoarse voice.

'You've got about half a minute to make

up your mind,' I said urgently. 'So make the most of it.'

Pai-Chang had descended the ladder to the boat some six feet below and now he was coming up again, his feet rattling the rungs. Pendlebury dropped to one knee behind me. There was the click of a knife-blade opening, a few quick movements and my bonds parted.

Pai-Chang came forward quickly, 'What's going on?'

He leaned down to peer closer in the dim light and I reached for his throat as I came up, which was a bad mistake for my hands were still numb and I couldn't exert any real strength. A grab at the throat is never to be advised if anything else will do as Pai-Chang demonstrated by clutching the lapels of my old Burberry, sticking a foot in my belly and tossing me over his head.

I went into the lake head first and had enough sense to stay under, turning and swimming beneath the jetty, surfacing cautiously on the other side. There was another ladder close to hand and I pulled myself out of the water very carefully and peered over the edge of the jetty.

Pendlebury was crouched on one knee on the

left, a look of complete terror on his face and Pai-Chang stood on the other side of the jetty peering into the dark waters, an automatic in one hand.

There was a boat hook hanging on a nail beside the ladder. I got one hand on it quickly and went over the edge of the jetty in a kind of rush. I went down on one knee, my foot slipping on the wet planking. He whirled round, gun ready. I lunged awkwardly at him with the boat hook, the only thing I could do, and caught him in the throat under the chin. He gave a short, stifled cry and went back into the water.

I poked around in the darkness with the end of the boat hook for a while, but it soon became obvious that he wasn't going to come up again. Pendlebury had slumped down to the wet planking and seemed to be crying, his face buried in his hands, shoulders heaving. I hauled him to his feet and gave him a shake.

'You can cut that out for a start. Where have they gone?' He hesitated rather obviously so I grabbed him by the throat. 'Suit yourself. I'd just as soon put you over the side to join your friend.'

'No, for God's sake, Jackson,' he gabbled. 'I'll tell you anything you want to know if only you'll promise to let me go.'

'All right,' I said. 'Start talking.'

'There's an island called Skerry about seven or eight miles off the Devon coast not far from Lundy. A group of Buddhist monks took the place over about four years ago. They were supposed to be refugees from Tibet, but they're part of Chen-Kuen's intelligence operations in Western Europe.'

'You're sure about this?'

He nodded vigorously. 'I've been there several times.'

'And that's where Chen-Kuen has gone now?'

'That's right. Connors Quay near Hartland Point is where he's making for.'

I thought about it all for a while standing there in the yellow light on the jetty with the rain falling. 'Did they leave the car I came in?'

'It's in the garage. Pai-Chang and I were supposed to leave in it after disposing of you.'

'Excellent.' I said. 'Let's get moving then.'

He backed away from me fearfully. 'You said I could go. You promised.'

'I know,' I said grimly, 'but then I'm a terrible liar. I intend to be at this place Connors Quay by morning and I've decided to take you with me, just to make sure you're telling the truth.'

There was nothing left in him at all after that and he collapsed completely, a broken man whose main difficulty was finding enough strength to place one foot in front of the other.

We were in the house for as long as it took me to help myself to dry clothes from his room and were on our way within a quarter of an hour.

Connors quay

8

I had some sort of wild notion that it might be possible to catch Chen-Kuen and his party before they reached their destination, but that was an utter impossibility as any sober examination of the facts indicated.

Connors Quay was the best part of a hundred miles from Sidbury, but in spite of the night and the weather, it was unlikely to take more than two and a half hours to get there and they had been on the way at least an hour and a half already.

It occurred to me that there might very well be some delay before they actually put to sea and suggested as much to Pendlebury.

'I'm not sure,' he said, 'but it's certainly a possibility. It would depend on the tide.'

'Why should that be?'

'It's the harbour on the island itself that's the trouble. You can only get in and out at high tide. It's the reefs, you see. The whole place is surrounded by them.'

'I see – and how many are there on this place at any one time?'

He seemed to come to life at that, turning sharply to look at me. 'Between forty and fifty, but I don't think you understand. They really are what they seem to be. Zen Buddhists. They lead a scrupulously religious life against a background of strict military training, just as in the old days. A man must be ready for all things, this is their philosophy.'

'A bloody fine way of peace they seem to enjoy.'

'But that's the conventional mistake of the Westerner. You entirely misconceive the whole philosophy. There is nothing wrong in fighting for what is good and desirable. In Japan, for example, most of the *samurai* were Zen disciples. The Zen way was the way for the warrior.'

'Communist-Buddhist monks,' I said. 'That's a new one.'

'Even Catholic priests fight the people's war in some South American countries,' he retorted. 'What about the Dominicans, for instance? More Marxist than the Marxists themselves. Isn't that what some people say?'

'All right,' I said. 'Roll on the day, only I'll make damn certain I'm not here to see it. I've had a bellyful of your lot and their philosophy. How in the hell did you get mixed up with them, anyway? I wouldn't have thought it was your life-style.'

'I first met Master Chen-Kuen many years ago when he was a student at the London School of Economics. I was lecturing in Fine Arts at the time and studying Zen as a disciple of an old Japanese master who had been living in London for some time. He introduced me to Chen-Kuen who helped me a great deal in the years that followed. I wrote several books and gained something of a reputation in the field.'

'And then he re-appeared and offered you the chance to run your own show at Sidbury?'

'How did you know that?' He seemed surprised, but didn't wait for an answer and simply carried straight on. 'The trouble is I'm weak.'

There was real pathos in his voice when he said that. 'My convictions have never gone very deep. I didn't like some of the things that I was drawn into, but by then it was too late. I had to do as I was told.'

'What particular piece of nastiness was he holding over your head? Young boys or public lavatories?'

I suppose I was being unnecessarily brutal under the circumstances for he flinched as if I had struck him and lapsed into silence. I suspect I was closer to the truth than I had realised.

Through Bridgwater and on to Taunton, I followed the narrow tunnel of light, darkness crowding in on either side. I drove alone with my thoughts for Pendlebury might as well have ceased to exist.

I went through it all then, starting with Tay Son and my first meeting with St Claire, Chen-Kuen, Madame Ny – it all came crowding back in extraordinary detail, clearer even than the events of the past few days.

Then there was Helen. It occurred to me with

something approaching guilt, that I hadn't really given her a great deal of thought. Hadn't even bothered to ask myself why Chen-Kuen had decided to take her with him unless she was to prove some sort of sop for her brother.

And what about St Claire? Had they passed him on already along the pipeline or was he still on the island? I think it was then that it occurred to me for the first time that if he was already on the high seas it would prove practically impossible to get him back.

Dawn seemed a long time in coming – grey and sombre, simply a lightening of the darkness and, in its place, a curtain of heavy rain so that when we drove through Bideford and took the coast road towards Hartland Point, it was impossible to see Lundy Island, so poor was the visibility.

Pendlebury had made no attempt to speak for some considerable time. In that grey light, his face was like a death mask, a look of complete desolation that in other circumstances might have made me feel sorry for him. He'd got into dark waters perhaps – gone in over his head and yet the cold, hard fact was that he had been prepared to act as agent in the small matter of my attempted murder. Five o'clock in the morning on the North Devon coast with the rain sweeping in from the Atlantic was no place for pity.

I found the sign for Connors Quay, turned into a narrow, winding road with hedges so high it was impossible to see over them and pulled into a small layby, cutting the engine. I lowered the window and breathed in the cold, morning air.

It was Pendlebury who spoke first, his voice as sombre as the morning. 'Mr Jackson, are you familiar with the Chinese expression *wu*?'

I nodded, 'The whole basis of Zen Philosophy. It roughly means acquiring a new viewpoint.'

He said, 'Or insight, if you like. What the Japanese term *satori*.'

'So what?'

'Sitting here at the tail-end of things for the past couple of hours with nothing to do except think, it has come to me, rather forcibly, that I have been wrong all these years. These are evil people and I have been part of that evil.'

'A little late in the day for that kind of talk.'

'Perhaps.' He smiled faintly. 'But not too late for me to offer my help.'

'And I'm supposed to believe that?'

'I hope you will, but any other attitude would be perfectly understandable.'

It was the voice that was the most impressive thing. Grave, serious and very calm, certainly nothing like the play-actor I had heard addressing the audience at the end of the service at the temple. None of which meant that I wasn't going to treat him with every caution.

I said, 'All right, outline the situation for me at Connors Quay for a start.'

'There was a quarry there years ago. They used to take the stone away by sea so there's quite a substantial pier. The whole place went into a decline at the turn of the century. It's private land now. Owned by the monks.'

'Do any of them live there?'

'No, there's only one habitable house left in the place. What used to be the village inn years ago. Davo lives there.'

'Who's he?'

'The rather unpleasant individual they employ

to look after things at this end. I think he's a Hungarian refugee. Came over after the rising in 1956. He runs their supplies across in a thirty-foot launch and sees that trespassers aren't made welcome.'

'Is there a telephone?'

'Yes, at the pub, but not to the island.'

'All right,' I said. 'Let's pay him a call, shall we?'

I took the Alfa down through that winding lane for another couple of miles and finally rolled to a halt at a five-barred gate which effectively cut off further progress. A large sign said *Private – keep out* and another *Warning – Guard Dogs Loose.* The gate itself had been secured with a heavy chain and two large padlocks.

'It's another quarter of a mile from here,' he said. 'We'll have to walk.'

'So it would appear. What about the dogs?'

'An empty threat. They don't exist in fact, but it keeps the holidaymakers away in the season.'

I decided on balance to believe him for he was, after all, going with me. We climbed over the gate and started downhill along a narrow, rutted track that followed a high hedge which to a certain extent broke the impact of the rain which was being driven in from the sea by the wind with some force now.

Pendlebury said nothing for a while and then caught my arm. 'From the next hedge you can see everything.'

Another five-barred gate which this time stood open and beyond, a hillside dropping steeply towards the inlet below. Half-a-dozen ruined cottages as he had said and the old pub, smoke rising from the chimney. Beyond, the pier running well out to sea into deep water, a tangle of rusting girders. There was a thirty-foot launch moored at the far end, but no sign of life as far as I could see. At least, not on deck, although it was difficult to be certain with the heavy rain and slight sea mist.

'There's a small stream about a hundred yards to the left,' Pendlebury said. 'It drops down to the back of the pub. We could approach unseen that way.'

Which seemed sensible enough and I followed him along the line of the hedge. He was limping heavily and his breathing wasn't all that it might have been, especially when we scrambled down into a gully and followed the stream where the going was considerably rougher.

His face was damp and not only from the rain when we climbed over the bank at the bottom and crouched behind a crumbling slate wall a few yards away from the back of the pub. There was a door to the yard, four windows at ground and first floor level, staring blindly into the grey morning, the smoke from the chimney the only sign of life.

I followed the wall round the side of the pub and peered over. A man was coming along the pier, perhaps a hundred yards away carrying a sack over his shoulder. He was dressed in sea boots, an old reefer jacket and cloth cap. I couldn't see his face for he had his head bowed against the rain.

Pendlebury said, 'That's Davo. Probably just returning from running them out to the island.'

'All right,' I said. 'Let's see if we can get inside before he arrives.'

We went through a small gate in the wall, crossed the yard and tried the back door. It was locked, in fact, looked as if it hadn't been opened in years. By then, it was too late to try anything else for Davo's voice was loud and clear now and not unpleasant. A slow, sad song to go with the weather and certainly not English although whether or not it was Hungarian I wasn't qualified to say.

'We'll let him get in, then we go round to the front and you knock on the door,' I told Pendlebury. 'Then get out of the way and leave the rest to me.'

His face sagged a little, but he didn't attempt to argue. We waited until the door banged and then made our move, following the wall round the side of the pub to the front.

There was still an old wooden sign swinging from a bar above the door, the colours vivid in the morning light. Scarlet and black mainly as befitted the subject. Death himself on a throne of corpses, the fleshless face beneath the crown, a cape of ermine falling from bony shoulders. *The Death of Kings* it was called.

I nodded to Pendlebury who was looking worried. He took a deep breath and started forward and I went after him, crouching to stay beneath the level of the windows. He glanced at me hesitantly, then knocked on the door.

There was a movement inside and then the door was opened cautiously.

Pendlebury forced a smile. 'Good morning, Davo.'

There was a grunt, surprise I suppose, and then the reply came. 'You? But I don't understand.'

For once, the lesser gods smiled on me for he stepped into the open and I saw that he was holding a Luger flat against his right thigh. He sensed my presence, started to turn as I booted him in the pit of the stomach. I gave him my knee in the face for good measure and put him flat on his back.

I picked up the Luger and put it in my pocket. Pendlebury was looking at me with something close to fear on his face. 'You never do things by halves, do you, Mr Jackson.'

'I could never see the point,' I said. 'Now let's get him inside.'

Davo's face was his most remarkable feature. Judas Iscariot to the life, one eye turned into the corner, the mouth like a knife slash. A face as repulsively fascinating as a mediaeval gargoyle.

We got him into a wooden chair by a deal table and I told Pendlebury to find me something to tie him with. He went out to the kitchen and returned with a length of clothes line. I lashed the Hungarian's wrists together behind the chair, then sat back and waited for him to recover.

This must have been the main room of the inn at one time. The floor was stone-flagged, the low ceiling supported by black oak beams and the stone fireplace was so large that there was an inglenook with a bench on either side.

There was a great driftwood fire burning there, warm and comfortable after the rawness outside, but even more interesting, a bottle of White Horse whisky on the table amongst the debris of what had presumably been last night's meal.

I poured some into a relatively clean cup, passed the bottle to Pendlebury and moved to the window to look outside. There was a telephone on the sill, Pendlebury had been telling the truth about that anyway. I swallowed some of my whisky and Davo groaned behind me.

He still didn't look too good so I went into the kitchen, filled a jug with cold water and threw it in his face. That brought him back to life with a jolt and he sat there cursing freely.

I slapped him back-handed just to get things off on the right foot which at least shut him up for a moment.

'That's better,' I said cheerfully. 'Now let's have a few answers. You've just taken Chen-Kuen and a party that included a young coloured woman across to Skerry. Am I right?'

Davo's bad eye rolled wildly as he turned his head to glare at Pendlebury. 'You're a dead man walking for this.'

I slapped him again, a little harder this time. 'I asked you a question.'

He spat in my face, hardly a pleasant sensation and certainly calculated to bring out the worst in me. There was an old three-foot iron poker standing in the hearth. I picked it up and shoved it into the flames. The abuse stopped with dramatic suddenness.

I said, 'During the past three days, I've been beaten up, drugged, committed to an institution for the criminally insane. We'll forget about the attempts on my life, they've become routine. I think you could say my patience has finally run out. I was trained in a hard school, my friend. Harder than you'll ever know. I'm going to wash my face and have another whisky, then I'll try some more conversation. The poker should be white-hot by then. Think about it.'

Pendlebury looked absolutely terrified and Davo's eyes rolled frantically as he strained against the chair. I went into the kitchen, ran the cold tap and splashed my face, then I returned to the living-room and poured another whisky. I took my time, rolling it around my mouth, more for effect than anything else for it was hardly the time of day to appreciate good Scotch.

I put down the cup and said calmly, 'Right, let's start again. You've just returned from delivering Chen-Kuen and a party that included a young coloured woman to Skerry. Am I right?'

He strained against his bonds with all his

strength, face contorted with the effort and the chair suddenly went over backwards. It must have been painful for his arms were pinned underneath and he stayed there, his body still tied to the chair in a sitting position. I walked to the fire, pulled out the poker and examined it. The end foot or so glowed white-hot, incandescent. I stood over him for a moment then touched it to the chair back. The wood actually burst into flame, paint sizzled, the smell immediately apparent.

He was tough but not that tough. He let out a yell that rattled the window frames. 'Yes, yes, you're right.'

'General St Claire – is he out there?' He frowned, fear and bewilderment mixed in his expression. 'A big man – a Negro. Quite unmistakable.'

He nodded frantically, his expression clearing. 'Yes, he came through the night before last.'

The relief was fantastic – so much so that I lowered my arm unthinkingly and the end of the poker touched the front of his jacket which flared at once.

'It's the truth,' he screamed. 'I swear it.'

I pursued my advantage. 'All right, what are they up to at the moment?'

'They're getting ready to leave.'

'Leave?' Pendlebury cut in. 'Who's leaving?'

'Everyone,' Davo said, 'I'm supposed to clear up here, then return to the island as soon as possible. We've got till nine-fifteen. They're getting the *Leopard* ready for sea now.'

I glanced at Pendlebury who said, 'The *Leopard*'s a sixty-foot ocean-going motor yacht. Panamanian registration.'

I turned back to Davo. 'What's her range?'

'Two thousand one hundred miles on full tanks at a cruising speed of twenty knots. She'll do thirty.'

Which made the whole thing about as bad as it could be. 'You said you'd got until nine-fifteen. What did you mean?'

'The tide drops like hell after that,' he said wearily. 'She'd never get over the reefs at the entrance. It's an excuse for a harbour at the best of times. The passage in through the rocks is only thirty feet wide.'

I tossed the poker into the fire, nodded to

Pendlebury and we lifted him upright again, still strapped into his chair.

Pendlebury said. 'What are you going to do? You can't stop them. It's too late.'

'Watch him,' I said and crossed to the telephone on the window sill.

He must have been sitting beside that phone biting his nails for I only got the ringing tone for a second and then the receiver was lifted.

'Morning, Sean,' I said. 'Was it worth it?'

'Ellis, for God's sake where are you? I came home at three a.m. to find all hell had broken loose at Marsworth Hall. You missing and Flattery, the night nurse, gone. I'd have been down there myself by now if it hadn't been for the message you left with the porter.'

So they still hadn't found Flattery and I wondered how many times that lift had been used since I left. There was a certain grim humour in the thought but it was hardly the time to go into it.

'Now listen carefully,' I said. 'Because I'm running out of time. Get in touch with Vaughan.

He's due in from Paris first thing. Tell him I've found St Claire.'

'You've what!'

'I'm phoning from a place called Connors Quay in North Devon, near Hartland Point. There's an island about eight miles offshore called Skerry. The place is inhabited by a colony of forty or fifty Zen Buddhist monks who are supposed to be Tibetan refugees and aren't.'

'And you say St Claire's there?'

'And his sister, only don't ask me to explain that one. I haven't got time. Tell Vaughan the man in charge is our old friend Colonel Chen-Kuen. He'll like that.'

There was a heavy silence. 'Look, are you getting all this down?'

'I don't need to. All my calls are tape recorded automatically.'

I said, 'Sean, I'm saner than I've been in months if that's what's worrying you and I haven't got time to argue the point. Chen-Kuen and his whole crowd intend to cut and run in a sixty-foot motor yacht called *Leopard* – Panamanian registration. They've only got till nine-fifteen. After that they lose the tide. You call Vaughan and tell him I'm going to hold the whole bloody crowd of them on that island till he gets there.'

'But how on earth can he manage in time?'

'Well, in Vietnam, we had a little item called the helicopter. I would have thought that the British Army, even allowing for its present depressed state, could run to two or three. And if the rest of these so-called monks are anything like the ones I've come across already, he'll need about half a company of the best assault troops he can lay his hands on. Over and out.'

I heard a final, urgent cry as I slammed down the receiver. When I turned, both Pendlebury and Davo were staring at me.

Pendlebury said, 'But this is madness. How can you hope to stop them on your own?'

'All I have to do is to prevent the *Leopard* from sailing until my friend Vaughan arrives with the cavalry.'

'And how can you possibly do that?'

'To use an apt, but rather inelegant English phrase, I'm going to block her passage.'

Out of the silence which followed, Davo said hoarsely, 'You're crazy.'

'I don't see why. We have a thirty foot wide outlet from that harbour from what you tell me and you have a thirty-foot launch at the end of the pier. The one should fit very nicely into the other, especially if we sink her in position.'

'You keep saying we,' Pendlebury said.

'I wouldn't dream of leaving you behind.' I produced the Luger and thumbed off the safety catch. 'All for one and one for all. That's my motto.'

Poor devil, he looked as if he might burst into tears at any moment, but not Davo. His face had hardened again, the eyes never left me. Now him, I would have to watch every step of the way.

The run to the island

9

The sea was choppy, rain squalls driven in towards the coast by a wind from the north-west and the old motor launch at the end of the pier bounced around at her moorings in a manner calculated to alarm all but the most experienced sailor.

We went down an iron staircase to the lower landing and down there, every sound seemed magnified, the waves booming beneath the lattice of rusting iron and receding again with great sucking sounds, reluctant and angry.

Pendlebury fell going over the rail, sprawling across a pile of stinking fishing nets. He staggered to his feet and looked across the inlet to the sea beyond where the waves were lifting into whitecaps, line upon line of them marching out of the mist and rain.

'You don't like it, eh?' Davo laughed hoarsely. 'Better get used to it. Likely to get worse before it gets better.'

I gave him a shove towards the wheelhouse. 'Get this thing moving. Try anything funny and I'll put a bullet through your knee-cap just for starters.'

There didn't seem much point in asking Pendlebury to help for he already looked about as ill as it was possible to be and squatted by the stern rail. I cast off from the deck for it suddenly occurred to me that the lines wouldn't be needed any more anyway.

The engines coughed into life at the same moment and as we left the shelter of the pier, waves started to slap against the hull and I could feel the vibration beneath my feet in the deck itself.

We heeled over as Davo increased speed and ploughed through that carpet of white water towards the mouth of the inlet. It was only when we actually moved out into open waters that the force of the wind was felt as great rain squalls thundered in towards the cliffs. The launch almost came to a dead halt, faltered, then started forward again as Davo increased power and the engine note deepened.

We ploughed on, bouncing across a continuous pattern of steep waves, water cascading across the deck. The wheelhouse was completely open to the stern deck and I stood to one side and hung on to a rail, the Luger ready in the other hand, close enough to Davo to watch what he was up to, but too far away to be rushed.

Pendlebury was sick over the rail a couple of times and finally staggered towards me. 'I think I'd better go below.'

'Nothing doing.' I gave him a push that sent him back to the pile of fishing nets. 'You stay there where I can keep an eye on you.'

Davo could handle a boat all right, I'll say that for him, for he varied his engine speed frequently to meet the constantly changing conditions in a way that showed he knew his business.

We were three miles out before we could see Skerry and the island was constantly obscured by rain as squall after squall raced in. Gradually things jumped into focus as we drew nearer. Black cliffs streaked with guano, breakers pounding in at their base.

Davo altered course and the other side of the island drifted into view, a great, rambling house standing in beech trees just below the rim of a hill, a Gothic monstrosity with mock turrets and so many chimneys it was impossible to count them. It had been built on the high tide of Victorian prosperity and a considerable amount of planting had been done at the same time, pine trees flooding up out of every gully and hollow.

The boat was rolling badly, so turbulent was the water. Davo hung on to the wheel, playing every trick of the current, but Pendlebury was in acute distress, sprawled across the nets, hanging on for dear life.

That particular squall raced past us and as we turned in towards the inlet below the house we were momentarily in quieter water.

Davo altered course another point. 'All right, what happens when we get there?'

I knew enough about small boat sailing to be on reasonably firm ground. I said, 'We take her in nice and easy. As soon as we're into the passage, cut the engine and I'll put the anchor over. Then we open the sea-cocks.'

'It won't work,' he said. There'll be one hell of a swell in there.'

'It better,' I said firmly. 'If she breaks through into the harbour there'll be a dead man at the wheel.'

He glanced sideways, that eye of his rolling again and saw from my face, I suppose, that I meant it.

'And what happens to us?'

'We swim for it.'

He shook his head. 'Not a chance without life-jackets.'

Which was reasonable enough. 'All right, where are they?'

'The locker behind you.'

I opened it, keeping a close eye on him, pulled three or four out and got one over my head, one-handed. When Pendlebury reached for another I stamped on his hand.

'Not yet – you two get yours at the right moment and only if you behave yourself.'

Davo's jaw tightened, but it was Pendlebury who reacted most strongly. 'But I can't swim, Jackson.'

His words were taken away as another squall

swept over the waves, rain bouncing across the deck like bullets. The boat yawed, almost turning broadside on. Davo fought to control her as a curtain of green water washed over us, sending Pendlebury across the deck into the starboard rail.

We were very close now, those black cliffs towering above us, birds wheeling in great clouds, razorbills, gulls, shags and a storm petrel swept low over the wheelhouse and up through the spray.

The sea was running in towards the inlet like a river in spate, turning over on itself constantly, washing over green-black rocks and I could see what he meant about the passage. A breakwater of giant blocks of masonry curved round on either side over the reef. The gap between was narrow enough to take the breath away.

But there was no time for qualms now – only action. He dropped his speed for the final run in and the sea caught us in its grip relentlessly.

Davo cried above the roaring, 'No good. I need more speed to control her.'

I held on tight with my left hand and raised the Luger, taking deliberate aim. 'I meant what

I said. Do exactly as I told you or I'll blow your head off.'

'But we'll all be killed,' Pendlebury screamed and then, as the boat rolled wildly and plunged in towards the passage he flung himself at me.

He clawed at my left arm and as I flung him away, Davo made his move, turning to grab at the Luger. I shot him twice in the body at point blank range, the force lifting him back against the side of the wheelhouse.

The wheel spun like a mad thing, the boat turned broadside on and the sea simply took us in its giant hand and tossed us into that narrow opening. I grabbed hard at the nearest rail with both hands out of sheer self-preservation, the Luger going its own way and a second later the launch smashed into the end of one of the piers.

The hull splintered like matchwood, the sea pulled us out again with a dreadful sucking sound the launch almost standing up on end and I rolled helplessly down the steeply inclined deck and went over the stern into the sea.

It was the life-jacket which saved me. I surfaced in time to see the launch swept in again, high on a crest that smashed it down hard across the rocks at the foot of the sea wall, the stern jutting out across the entrance to the harbour.

Not quite what I had intended, but just as effective. Men were running along the wall now, saffron robes vivid against the grey. They weren't going to be pleased with what they found, but that didn't concern me. I had other things to think about.

I was caught in a current of considerable strength that took me away from the harbour in a great curve, bearing me out beyond the point and round to the other side parallel to the shore and perhaps fifty yards out.

On such a course, I could inevitably drift past the island altogether into the wide Atlantic, America next stop, but it was not to be for with something of an anti-climax, the current changed course abruptly, swinging in towards a wide bay at the foot of the cliffs.

Not that I was to be let off too lightly. A wall of water, green as bottle glass, smashed down on me, driving me under the surface. I went deep, too deep, fighting for life like a fish on a hook.

I surfaced in a sea of white water, gasping for air and went under again as another wall of water rushed in. My foot kicked sand or shingle, something solid at any rate and I found myself sprawling across a great, round boulder streaming with water, seaweed all around.

Another wave bowled me over. My hands found a jagged edge of rock, held on fast. As the sea receded again, I lurched forward across the rocks, stumbling like a drunken man and fell on my face on a strip of the softest, purest, whitest sand I have ever known at the base of the cliffs.

The sea still roared inside my head when I stood up, the earth moved beneath my feet which was hardly surprising. I got the life-jacket off, pushed it down out of sight behind some stones, then examined the cliffs.

They were nothing like as perpendicular as they had seemed from the sea, sloping gently backwards at one point, cracked and fissured by great gullies. It was an easy enough climb and I emerged on a round shoulder of rock about a hundred feet above the beach within five or six minutes. From there it was no more than a strenuous scramble over grass and tilted slabs of black stone. I slowed to approach the edge with caution perhaps ten minutes after leaving the beach.

I found myself twenty or thirty yards from the edge of a stand of pines. There didn't seem to be anyone about so I put down my head and ran for cover.

It was quiet in there as pine woods often are, the trees crowding closely together, their branches intermingled so that not much of the rain was managing to get through. I paused to catch my breath, then started to move in the general direction of the harbour.

Within a couple of minutes I was able to see the house and then the trees started to peter out which made things awkward for there was a good fifty yards of clear ground to the nearest point from which I would be able to see down into the inlet, and yet I had to know what was going on down there.

A slight fold in the ground provided me with some sort of cover and took me half-way. I crawled from that point through the wet grass, not that it made much difference for I was soaked to the skin already.

The view from the edge was more than interesting. The launch was hard on the rocks at the base of the breakwater, her stern partially under the water, but virtually blocking the entrance. There were at least two dozen monks down there and others running down the twisting road from the house to join them.

Several were at the edge of the breakwater directly above the boat, obviously making an attempt to assess the situation. The *Leopard* was tied up to a jetty well inside the harbour where the water was comparatively calm, a beautiful boat in blue and white that looked capable of crossing the Atlantic if necessary.

There was a sudden commotion amongst the monks, voices drifted up, blown by the wind. They clustered at the edge of the breakwater above the rocks, someone produced a rope. I saw it snake out over the edge, presumably to the rocks to one side of the launch which were out of my sight.

One of the monks went over himself. There

was a short pause, then several laid hands on the line. After a while, Rafe Pendlebury appeared.

They had him on his back for some time, working in relays, obviously pumping the water out of him and then a rather startling thing happened. There was a clattering of hooves and I glanced up to see three or four monks riding down from the house, mounted on what looked like sturdy Welsh mountain ponies. The most interesting thing was that Chen-Kuen was in the lead.

As the crowd parted on the breakwater to let him through, the men working over Pendlebury hauled him into a sitting position and one of them started to thump him vigorously in the back. Chen-Kuen dismounted and crouched beside him.

None of this, of course, made the future any too bright as far as I was concerned, for whichever way you looked at it, once he'd heard Pendlebury's story, he'd come looking for me, hoping with all his heart that I had survived to reach the shore so that he could see to me himself.

It was time to get moving, but to where? It

was obvious that they'd be starting to scour the island within minutes, particularly this section of the cliff. I think it was then, as I started back towards the line of trees, that it occurred to me that the safest place to be during the next couple of hours might be the house itself, or at least within its grounds. Certainly the last place they would consider looking for a while.

Which meant getting there while most of them were still down on the breakwater. I ran into the shelter of the trees, pushing my way through the close knit branches towards the far side for it had become apparent to me that this particular section stretched on a course parallel with the shape of the cliffs above the inlet, dropping down behind the house itself. If I kept to the trees all the way, it would take forever, but once through to clear ground on the other side and using them as a shield, I could make much faster progress.

God, but it was a tangle and I pushed through, head-down, branches tearing at my head. As I neared the edge, I heard a horse whinny, the stamp of hooves and paused, going on with extreme caution. It was only a herd of twenty or thirty of those shaggy mountain ponies, grazing together in a tight group – or so I thought.

As I moved into the open, two or three of the ponies nearest to me shied, setting the whole herd stamping nervously. I started to run along the edge of the trees and immediately became aware of the drumming of hooves in the rear.

Presumably he'd been acting as some sort of herdsman, though God knows where he'd been hiding – probably sheltering from the rain in the trees at the edge of the wood. He certainly looked the part for he was wearing a great sheepskin *shuba* belted at the waist, a garment habitually worn by Tibetan monks in cold weather and a conical sheepskin hat with ear flaps.

I made it into the trees with a final lung-bursting rush. He almost had me, but amongst those closely packed pines, he was at something of a disadvantage. The strange thing was that he didn't seem to be carrying a gun, only a sword with an ivory handle which hung under his left armpit, suspended by a sling from around his neck. He drew it suddenly, urging the pony on, slashing at the branches before him to clear his way.

He was perhaps three or four yards to my rear and I turned suddenly, doubled back to the left of him, ran in from the side, grabbed his foot and heaved him from the saddle.

There was a certain amount of confusion for a few moments after that. I flung myself under the pony's belly, one hand reaching for the herdsman's throat, the other for his sword-hand for he'd hung on to that tight enough.

Not that he could do much damage with it in those circumstances for it was a good three feet long, curving wickedly – an excellent specimen of the ancient Chinese blade of which the Japanese *samurai* sword is a copy. A terrifying weapon in the hands of a trained *kendo* swordsman, but not much use when threshing about on the ground at close quarters.

In any case, I chopped him across the throat with the edge of my hand the moment I got close which quietened him effectively enough.

The pony was certainly well trained for he had stopped dead a yard or two away and stood waiting, pawing the ground nervously with one hoof. I thought about it for at least one full second, then did what seemed the obvious thing and started to undress my friend on the floor.

The sheepskin *shuba* and the hat with the ear flaps were all that I needed for, although they both stank abominably, they would provide me with as effective a disguise as I could wish for, at least at a distance.

I took his sword, sheathed it and slipped the sling over my neck. He was still alive when I left him although I must admit he didn't look good. But I had other things on my mind as I grabbed the pony's bridle and pushed him on through the trees into the open.

I urged him up the slope on a course diagonal to the line of the trees. Immediately, the whole herd of ponies came after me, several streaking past, heads down. The rain blew in from the sea in great gusting clouds. Cutting visibility, so that it was something of a shock when a number of horsemen streamed over the crest of the hill and galloped along the skyline.

They were half-obscured by the rain, yellow robes vivid against the grey like something out of an old Chinese water colour painting. I raised one hand in a half-salute and kept on going, thankful that the ponies had chosen to follow me. The riders faded to the left and I went over the crest and plunged down towards the trees at the back of the house.

The ponies milled around me, pushing and snorting, the smell of them heavy on the damp air as I jumped to the ground. I smacked my mount hard across the rump sending it cantering back the way we had come. The others followed and I moved into the trees.

A grey stone wall about five feet in height divided the woods from the gardens surrounding the house. I scrambled over and dropped into the clump of rhododendrons. Everything was in excellent order, leaves raked into symmetrical piles, paths tidied, grass neatly trimmed. All as I would have expected in a place run by people who looked upon work of any description as being not only a moral obligation, but an act of worship.

I worked my way closer to the house which was not particularly difficult for the banks of rhododendrons gave excellent cover. I finally halted in the shelter of an old summer house.

It had the general air of decay common to such places long disused. Rain drifted in through a broken pane of glass, cobwebs glistened in each dark corner. A faint uneasy stirring, a memory of childhood perhaps as I crouched there.

Poor little Ellis Jackson taking on the whole world again. I managed some sort of a smile at that one and got to my feet. I could stay where I was, keep under cover till Vaughan and his men arrived or try the house, which was certainly the most interesting prospect.

It seemed to be waiting for me, crouched there in the rain. If I was going to make a move, it would have to be a bold one, so I stood up, walked briskly along the path till I came to the courtyard at the rear of the building. I pulled the sheepskin cap down as far as it would go and started across.

When I was half-way there, the door opened, I veered sharply to my left, walking at exactly the same pace towards what looked like the stable block. I was aware of two monks emerging from the door. I kept on going. The entrance to the stable block was a great iron-bound door, obviously large enough to allow a carriage through, but there was the usual judas gate set in it and I stepped inside.

There were entrances off the tunnel to left and right containing rows of stalls. I could smell the ponies, hear the odd stamp as an animal moved nervously. The tunnel emptied into a large central hall with a domed roof which had presumably been either a carriage house or, more probably, an indoor riding school at one time.

That it was now used for a different purpose was perfectly obvious. There were rifle racks along one wall containing not only AK47s but several M16s, ammunition belts complete with bayonets in scabbard and a couple of M79 grenade launchers which I presumed were just for show until I noticed the belts of grenades hanging from pegs above them.

Even more interesting was the row of life-sized dummies hanging in a line parallel with the rear wall, each one a replica of an American G.I. right down to his jungle green fatigues. They had all been bayoneted dozens of times.

I helped myself to an AK47, loaded it and buckled an ammunition belt about my waist, then moved back along the tunnel to the main entrance and opened the door cautiously. The courtyard was deserted, so I stepped out and crossed to the house again.

The rear door opened into a dark, stone-flagged corridor of the type usually found in a house of that sort leading from the kitchens to the residential area.

I moved along it cautiously, pausing at a green baize door at the far end, the kind you find only in England and nowhere else. It went with weekend house parties, tinkling ice in tall glasses, people seeking a fourth for bridge. I stifled an insane desire to laugh as I put my ear to that door and listened.

I tried it carefully, peering out through the crack and looked into a fairly large hall floored with black and white Dutch tiles, a wide oak staircase giving access to the second floor.

But at that, the resemblance to any other English country house faded. The walls were hung with dragon tapestries and the niche which had probably been originally intended for an Italian marble statue now contained the usual gold-painted figure of Buddha and the air was heavy with the smell of the incense that burned in the brass bowl in front of it.

I hesitated, debating whether to carry straight on or not when an astonishing thing happened. A door opened in the gloom of the corridor on the far side and Helen St Claire appeared.

She was dressed exactly as I had last seen her in slacks and sweater. She looked tired, very tired, and clenched and unclenched her hands nervously. I noticed that particularly.

The two Chinese with her wore dark trousers and Guernsey sweaters and each had an ammunition belt, twin to my own, strapped about his waist and carried an assault rifle. They went up the main staircase. I waited until they reached the landing and went after them.

The main corridor was deserted when I got up there myself, but there were voices talking in Chinese at the other end. A moment later, I heard someone coming and barely had time to dodge into a small dead-end corridor out of sight. One of the two guards went past and descended the stairs quickly. I gave him a moment or so to get out of the way, then started along the corridor in search of Helen.

When I peered round the corner at the end, I found the other guard standing outside a mahogany door. I didn't really get much chance to consider what to do next – it was decided for me by the man himself turning his back to peer out of a nearby window. Such a chance was obviously not to be misused so I stepped close behind him and tried a simple *shime-waza*, a strangle hold which clamped across his carotid artery and had him unconscious in seconds.

I left him there on the floor for the moment for there wasn't much else I could do and tried the door handle, the AK ready for action under one arm, finger on the trigger. The door opened gently and I slipped inside.

It was an airy, rather pleasant room with pale yellow wallpaper, white curtains billowing in the breeze from the open window. There was a bed in one corner and a desk over by the window. Helen St Claire stood in front of it – her brother sat behind.

In a way, it was as if she ceased to exist for a moment. He sat there staring at me dressed in the same kind of Guernsey sweater as the guards only a size too small, a look of utter astonishment on his face.

'Oh, no, Ellis,' I heard Helen say.

And then he smiled, that famous St Claire smile that made him unique, himself alone and like no other man on top of the earth – and jumped to his feet, the chair falling backwards.

'Well, damn me, boy, but it's about time.'

'I'd have thought you long gone by now,' I said. 'They must have put something in your tea.'

But they hadn't if the way he came round that desk in a rush was anything to go by. It was Tay Son all over again and I was more pleased to see him than I would have thought possible.

I put out my hand to meet his and, when he was close enough, he kicked me in the stomach with everything he had and I went down like a tree falling.

Black max

10

I didn't lose consciousness – simply fought for air as I writhed on the floor, the centre of a dark agony, eyes tight shut. Helen was on her knees beside me, I was aware of that because I could smell her perfume, recognise that cool hand. As for St Claire, there was no answer to that – not for the moment – none that made sense.

When I opened my eyes, the faces above me were a meaningless blur. I closed them again, felt myself being picked up and carried across the room to be dumped in a chair.

After a while my mouth was forced open and brandy poured down my throat. Only a little, but it burned and I started to cough. A hand pounded me between the shoulder blades and St Claire laughed.

'Keep going, boy, you'll make it.'

I surfaced again and found him sitting on the edge of the desk. He grinned, a kind of admiration on his face and shook his head. 'Christ, Ellis, but you're indestructible.'

I ignored him and turned to Helen who was standing at the other end of the desk, nothing but despair on her face. 'Are you all right?' I asked her.

She simply dissolved into tears, something I had never known her do before, sobbing helplessly, her whole body shaking. St Claire went to her at once, gathered her into those great arms, stroked her hair and spoke in a low, soothing voice, words that I could not hear.

I threw a quick glance over my shoulder to discover the other guard standing there, clutching a machine pistol, so any ideas I might have had about making a run for it were smartly nipped in the bud. In any event, at the same moment, the door opened and Chen-Kuen entered. He wore untanned leather riding boots, a saffron robe that fell just below his knee and a quilted, wide-sleeved *shuba* over it in black. Completely mediaeval, imposing, vital looking, he dominated the room instantly.

He nodded to St Claire. 'Take her next door, Max. I'll send for you when I want you.'

St Claire did exactly as he was told, going out instantly, one arm about his sister's shoulders.

Chen-Kuen told the guard to wait outside, speaking in Chinese this time, then sat on the edge of the desk and looked at me, a slight frown on his face, of concern more than anything else. His right hand, I noticed, was inside his robe.

'Are you all right?'

'I'll survive.'

He smiled at that. 'One must admit you seem to have a flair for doing just that. There is a Zen saying: When a lioness gives birth to cubs, after three days she pushes them over a cliff to see if they can get back.'

'To hell with that kind of talk,' I said. 'Let's have some facts. I'd say I've earned them. As St Claire obviously isn't here under any kind of duress, I presume he's been working for you?'

'Exactly.' He sat down behind the desk and helped himself to a cigarette from an ivory box, his right hand still inside the robe.

There was a kind of iron band around my

head that seemed to be squeezing tighter by the second. The pain was quite intense so that thinking, clear, rational thinking at any rate, which was what I needed now, was extraordinarily difficult.

I said, 'So that's why he had to die? Presumably because they were finally on to him?'

He nodded. 'And dead, or at least supposed dead, he would have been rather more use to us, as I'm sure you will understand.'

'Are you trying to tell me he broke out there in Tay Son? That you had your way with him?' I shook my head. 'No, that isn't possible. I was there. I was with him. I knew what was happening.'

'My dear Ellis, if you mean did I succeed in brainwashing him into becoming a dedicated Marxist, the answer is no. It was not possible with his psychological type and there was no need.'

'I don't understand.'

'It's simple enough. To use a popular American phrase, St Claire's one great need is to be where the action is. To hold the centre of the stage. To perform violent, spectacular deeds, to live dangerously. Call it what you will. Strangely enough in view of his past – I refer mainly to his military record now – he does not need an audience, but he does have an obsessional need for danger and excitement. Obsession, as you know, may take many forms. Various kinds of sexual aberration, for example, strange needs which simply cannot be denied by the subject.'

'And you're trying to tell me that St Claire has just as total an obsession for action, violence and so on?'

'It explains his whole life. There is, of course, an element of self-destruction involved, suicidal, if you like, which he fails to recognise himself. I discovered all this quite early in our relationship at Tay Son. The rest was easy.'

The whole had been delivered in a careful academic tone as if he were back at university holding a tutorial or seminar.

I said, 'You'll have to spell it all out for me.'

'He was dead, Ellis. To the world outside, he had been killed in action. I pointed this out to him. Told him he would be sent to China and held in solitary confinement for the rest of his days.'

'And the alternative was to agree to work for you?'

'Exactly – to go back to the outside world, a hero if possible and work for us.'

'But he didn't need to do it,' I said. 'How could you possibly guarantee that he would play the game your way once he was free?'

'It was worth the chance. To discredit him would have been simplicity itself.' He shrugged. 'We could have released tape recordings of various conversations, signed documents, that sort of thing. Even if all these had been dismissed as a communist plot, the mud would have stuck. He would have been finished in real terms. Still employed by the army perhaps for the sake of appearances, but in some backwater job of that type that would have driven a man like him out of his mind. In any case, there was no need for threats. He began to enjoy it, Ellis. He discovered that it was, as you English say, just his cup of tea. A new thrill, if you like, for a man who had tried everything else there was to try. To pit his wits against the intelligence departments of every country in the NATO alliance, which was what he was eventually doing. To make fools of them all.'

'Only some of the time presumably.'

He shook his head. 'No, he was quite brilliant, I must give him that although I have always detested the man. In the end he was betrayed by a defector from our own side. Even then, both the CIA and British intelligence discounted the suggestion as a fabrication at first.'

So even Vaughan had been less than honest with me? Poor little Ellis Jackson indeed. I was beginning to feel rather angry, but there was one thing I still had to know. In a way, the most important item of all.

I said, 'Where did I fit in to all this? Way back, I mean?'

'In Vietnam?' He nodded. 'I wondered when you would get round to that. You were used from the beginning, I should imagine that must have got through to you by now. Frankly, Ellis, you were something of a godsend to us. Exactly the right man at the right time. We were doubly lucky in that your psychological pattern, which I'm sure you'll be the first to agree is hardly normal, was just right. Black Max was exactly what you needed and you, in turn, were exactly the right companion for his spectacular escape. You confirmed to the world so beautifully what a hero he'd been – how he had stood firm against everything they'd done to him.'

I was surprised I could still talk. 'And later, when he found me in London again?'

'By design – all arranged. He always thought you might be useful so he persuaded me to provide you with just what you needed – Sheila Ward.'

'Another Madame Ny?'

'If you like. She was killed in Hanoi in an air raid six months ago, by the way, if you're still interested.'

'She can rot in hell for all I care.'

I shouted at him, hands clenched, taking a quick step forward. His hand came out of the robe holding some sort of automatic pistol.

I said, 'Do you want to know something rather funny? I always rather liked you.'

'And I you. Nothing personal, Ellis, you

understand that. I have my duty. I serve a great cause. The greatest in the world. The people's cause.'

'Always your bloody cause,' I said. 'You're all the same, both sides of the bloody fence, nothing to choose between you.' I laughed in his face. 'You've lost out this time, by God, at least I'll have that consolation.'

'I don't think so. Friend Pendlebury came ashore on the rocks by the breakwater so I know all about your telephone call to London – the time element involved.' He got to his feet and walked to the window. 'You tried, Ellis, and you lost. See for yourself.'

There were about forty of them down there heaving on a double line which snaked over the breakwater and was presumably attached to the wrecked launch and the *Leopard* was manoeuvring her way into the outlet channel, obviously with the idea of trying a little pushing.

'We'll be on our way within half-an-hour, all of us.' He patted me on the shoulder. 'You'll go with us, of course. I was foolish to leave you behind at Sidbury. Your particular virtues are hard to come by. We'll find a use for you, never fear. And now I must go down to the harbour to hurry them along.'

I really did think that I was going crazy then. I suppose it was his calmness, the cool assumption that having realised I had lost, I would be a good boy from now on and do the sensible thing.

He opened the door and as he went out, the guard stepped back in. The door closed and I returned to the window and looked down at the harbour. As I watched, the launch actually moved, the stern lifting out of the water and the *Leopard* started to inch forward.

Behind me, the door opened and, when I turned, St Claire stood there, Helen at his shoulder.

In that first moment, in that one fixed point in time I could have killed him – would have done if a gun had come to hand and Chen-Kuen's words returned to haunt me. *Black Max* was exactly what I had needed, wasn't that what he had said? Not Brigadier-General James Maxwell St Claire, but Black Max, every boy's fantasy figure. The father I'd never known. There, it was out.

And I think he knew something had broken deep inside for his face, when he came forward, was deadly serious.

He raised a hand as if he thought I would rush him. 'Let's get one thing straight, Ellis. Helen knew nothing about it. Okay?'

'I loved you, do you know that?' It was a howl of agony straight up from my guts. 'You were everything I never had. A god on earth. And you used me. You never gave a damn from the first to the last. You stood by while they set me up for a criminal lunatic – tried to drive me clean out of my wits.'

His eyes widened in utter astonishment and in that single tiny moment of truth, I saw into the heart of the man. The tremendous ego that made him incapable of seeing anything in any other terms except those of self. No love here, not for anyone, even Helen, certainly not for me and perhaps not even for himself in the final analysis.

And now came the attempt at self-justification. 'You know what happens when you get the

Congressional? Well, I'll tell you, boy. That's it.' He made a cutting motion through the air between us. 'Finish. All washed-up. I'd rather be you than me, says the President. Your country loves you. No more action for you, boy. No, not ever.'

'What's this supposed to be, an excuse?' I yelled.

'I sat on my arse in the Pentagon for five years after Korea. Five more at Staff College, instructing. When that chance came to go to Vietnam as a member of the President's own commission. To smell a little powder again . . .'

I punched him in the mouth with all my strength, hard enough to rock even him, sending him staggering back into the guard at the door.

The whole thing had been quite unpremeditated, a completely spontaneous gesture of rage and frustration, but the results were more than I could have hoped if the whole thing had been by design.

St Claire lost his footing and cannoned into the guard who grabbed frantically at the wall in an effort to keep his balance and succeeded in dropping his rifle in the process. A hound dog couldn't have descended on a rabbit any faster than I snapped up that AK. I drove the butt into the side of the guard's skull and rammed the muzzle into St Claire's face as he scrambled on to one knee.

Helen gave a terrible cry, a hand to her mouth, imagining I suppose, that I would kill him there and then. She rushed in at me and I sent her back against the wall with a stiff right arm.

'I'm leaving now,' I told St Claire, 'And I'm taking her with me. If you want me and I think I can assure you you will, I'll be waiting out there in the woods somewhere. When you come looking, we'll see just how good you really are.'

He opened his mouth to speak and I reversed the rifle and struck him a heavy blow in the side of the neck with the butt.

Helen opened her mouth to cry and as he slumped to the floor, I slapped her heavily across the face. 'None of that. You do exactly as you're told from now on, understand me?'

I shoved her out into the corridor ahead of me and closed the door.

I think that was the beginning of a kind of

madness, a black, killing rage. Utter humiliation was the root cause, I suppose. All my life I had never known what it was to have a real relationship with anyone. Sold down the river at every turn. Madame Ny, Sheila Ward, and now Black Max St Claire. Poor little Ellis Jackson indeed. Well, we'd bloody well see about that.

If anyone had tried to stop me, I'd simply have shot my way through, but the house was quiet as we went down the stairs, everyone, I suppose, being down at the breakwater helping with the launch. I ran across the yard to the stable block, dragging her behind me by the hand. As I shoved her ahead of me, she was sobbing hysterically.

I went straight to the weapon racks and helped myself to an ammunition belt complete with bayonet which I buckled about my waist after checking that I'd got the right one. Next I draped two belts of grenades around my neck and slung one of the M79 grenade launchers over my shoulder.

Helen had sunk down on the floor against the wall apparently exhausted. I hauled her to her feet and shook her. 'Come on, let's get moving.'

She seemed completely bewildered. 'But I don't understand. What can you possibly hope to do on your own?'

'Show these bastards how to fight a war,' I said and I picked up an AK assault rifle and pushed her towards the door.

I followed the same route out as I had used on the way in, through the rhododendron bushes and over the stone wall to the meadow beyond.

From then on, something happened that can't be explained in purely physical terms. It was as if I had forgotten what fatigue was and was possessed of limitless energy. I ran across that meadow towards the pine trees without flagging, dragging her behind me and when we reached their shelter, it was Helen who sobbed for breath.

I suppose I'd gone berserk in a way, just like the old Norsemen and a furious energy bubbled up inside me, God knows from where.

I pushed Helen along in front of me through the trees and she cried out in pain as branches flailed at her face, but I had no time for pity. When we came out on the other side, there was the usual twenty or thirty yards of open ground to the edge of the cliff. I dragged her down on her hands and knees and made her crawl like an animal, great sobs tearing at her throat, towards an outcrop of rock on a small point a few yards away.

It sloped upwards, no more than three feet off the ground at the highest point, forming a natural breastwork and beyond was the inlet.

I laid out the AK and several clips of ammunition. Next came the M79 and lastly, the two pouches of six grenades each. I pushed Helen down flat and peered over the edge of the rock.

I wasn't a moment too soon. The combined efforts of the monks hauling on the lines and the *Leopard* using her prow as a ram had almost succeeded in their object. The launch had been pushed partially away from the gap between the two breakwaters. The *Leopard* was almost through although she was being thrown about in the heavy swell.

I slithered back down the rock and extracted the first grenade from its pouch. To my horror, it was a smoke grenade designed to be fired by the M79, but no earthly use for my purpose. The other belt contained what I was seeking, which was something, although I was now reduced to six instead of the twelve I had intended.

The M79 grenade launcher is breech-loading and in a way, resembles a sawn-off shot-gun. It fires a rather lethal cartridge-type grenade with high fragmentation on impact. I wasn't too sure about the range from here, but the height I was firing from would help considerably. I shoved one up the spout, aimed for the *Leopard*, resting the barrel on the edge of the rock and fired.

I could actually follow the progress of the grenade through the air. It overshot the *Leopard* and landed on the rocks behind the launch. The effect was all that I could have wished for. A couple of monks fell over the edge of the breakwater and pieces of the launch's hull lifted lazily into the air.

But it was the *Leopard* I was after and I had missed. I remembered the old deer-stalking maxim from boyhood, the general at his best and teaching me to shoot. *Always aim high when firing downhill.*

The second grenade landed between the

breakwater and the *Leopard*, the explosion putting a hole in her hull the size of a house door. The third bounced on the stern and the deck disintegrated in a great scarlet mushroom as the fuel tank exploded.

She sank like a stone a few seconds later.

It had all happened so quickly, this thunderbolt descending, that those on the breakwater were still in utter confusion. I had no time to look for Chen-Kuen personally, just hoped that he was down there as I aimed another grenade on the breakwater itself.

It took out six or seven monks at one fell swoop, bodies hurtling backwards into the harbour. They certainly scattered after that. The fifth grenade did nothing like as much damage. It was round about then that shots started to come back in our direction so I dropped the M79 and tried the AK47.

Most of the monks were running up the hill towards the house. I picked off a couple who were well up in front and that really did it. Men scattered in all directions. Within a couple of minutes, there didn't really seem to be anyone left on view at all.

After that, the bullets started to fly thick and fast. I think I knew from the beginning that such a position would not really be tenable for very long. What really decided me was Helen. She had been lying crouched close to the earth, her face turned towards me, absolutely terrified.

Now, she gave a sudden sharp cry and clapped a hand to her cheek. It was either a ricochet or perhaps a splinter of rock, but in any event, she had a nasty gash, bone-deep, blood pouring through her fingers.

I slung the grenade launcher over my shoulder, the pouches around my neck, grabbed her by the arm and ran for the cover of the woods.

SEEK AND DESTROY

11

Helen was in no condition to go anywhere, but I urged her on, following the line of the woods for a couple of hundred yards or so, but it was no good. She just didn't have the strength and constantly stumbled so that it was a physical effort to keep her upright.

We cut through the trees and paused beside a low stone wall. Somewhere not too far away, I heard voices calling, the sound of hoofbeats.

The game was afoot with a vengeance for they were hopelessly trapped on this island till Vaughan got here. Nowhere to run. Nothing to do except run Ellis Jackson into the ground. Well, if that's what they wanted, they could have it. I'd been in worse places and survived.

With a sudden rush, a dozen or so horsemen cantered over the hill to the right and crossed our field of vision. They were all wearing monk's robes except for St Claire who was in the lead, mounted on a pony like the rest although it seemed ridiculously small for him.

Helen moaned as if about to cry out and I got a hand to her mouth to close it. The hoofbeats faded into the rain and I released her.

The blood on her cheek was congealing now. She fumbled in her pocket and found a handkerchief which she rolled into a pad and held against the wound.

'All right,' I said. 'Let's move out.'

She said weakly, 'Even now, here at the final end of things, you can't tell the difference between fantasy and reality. You still believe you can take on the whole world and win.'

'It's all I've had to hang on to since I was eight years old. Now get on your bloody feet and move.'

I pulled her up and shoved her in front of me, pushing her into a stumbling run, out into the open across the meadow for that fringe of pine wood at the edge of the cliff above the inlet was one place they would turn inside out. To venture into open country would be unlooked for and it is the unexpected that succeeds in war. We laboured up to the crest of the hill and I pushed her down into a small hollow and crouched beside her.

They were calling now on every side down there in the hollow, beating through the trees to flush me out like a shooting party out for a morning's sport.

Beyond the crest of the slope on which we lay there was a long, sloping hillside of sparse grass, no cover anywhere, but on top was a circle of stones, one of those legacies of the Bronze Age so common in the west country. It was obvious standing out there for the whole world to see on top of that mound and therefore the last place they would think of looking, or so it seemed to me then.

I said to Helen, 'Take a deep breath and get ready to run. We've got about three hundred yards to go. I don't want to end up by dragging you by your hair, but I will if I have to.'

She made no comment, simply got to her feet and stumbled forward, clutching the handkerchief to her cheek. We were in maximum danger all the way of course – completely in the open

– no place to hide if anyone should appear. It needed luck and we got it, for suddenly the wind started to drive the rain in across the cliffs again in great solid sheets, cutting down visibility considerably.

We made it into the standing circle and dropped down into cover and, below, the wind ripped rain and mist away to disclose more horsemen on the fringe of the woods.

'That's what I call timing,' I told her.

She crouched against one of the standing stones, the pad to her face, the eyes very wide and filled with pain. 'You could have killed Max down there – picked him off as he rode past. Why didn't you?'

'I'm saving him for later.'

I rammed a full clip into the AK. She said in a hoarse voice, 'What kind of man are you to kill so easily – so terribly?'

'Ask him,' I said. 'Ask Black Max. He made me what I am if anyone did.'

She shook her head. 'No, I can't accept that. Each man is responsible for his own destiny.'

'I bet that sounds good in those lectures you give at the Sorbonne. Does it excuse your brother's conduct, by the way? Murderer, renegade, traitor. Or didn't he tell you?'

She broke down completely then and slid to the ground, her face pillowed in the wet grass. She would never be able to condemn him, I saw that now – had always known, I suppose. She loved the man – worshipped him with every fibre of her being. To have suggested that love was possibly incestuous would have been to make it entirely too superficial. This thing went far beyond that.

And yet I could feel no pity. I was long past that. I wanted to see them all in hell – to suffer as I had suffered. As for St Claire, it seemed to me then that thirty years of some kind of penal servitude or other would do very well – the least they'd give him. A bullet would be much too easy.

I wanted all these things so much that I could taste them and as I have said, I think that by then, I was more than a little mad – hardly surprising in view of what had happened. I gazed up into the grey morning praying for Vaughan and somewhere a pony whinnied.

There was a group of them crossing the curve

of the hill half-way down, their voices clear. I slid the AK forward, ready for action, motioning Helen to silence.

They kept on going at a fast trot and then it happened. One man at the rear wheeled his pony out of line and cantered up towards the standing circle.

Even then, at the end of things, I held off, waiting, hoping that he might turn away. He reined-in a yard or two away, a young man, rain beading his face, a black and scarlet band tied firmly around his forehead, the ends hanging down a couple of feet at the rear. His only weapon was one of those three-foot swords slung under his arm in an ivory sheath.

I think it was then that I realised what was happening – saw the affinities with the *samurai* code. He was a warrior, ready to die with honour in the old way, the only way for a man – sword in hand. The band around his head was obviously similar to the *samurai* death band, worn by those who seek to die in the face of the enemy.

It may seem crazy, all this, yet subsequent events proved me to be entirely right. It was as if this was all they had left – to seek and destroy the man who had destroyed them – to hunt him down in their own way.

He started to turn his pony, then wheeled suddenly. I don't know what it was he had seen, but it was enough. His mouth opened in a terrible cry to fill his limbs with courage, to bring the *ch'i* up from his belly, the sword flashed and he jumped the pony over the crest of the slope into the circle.

I rolled on my back as Helen screamed and lifted him out of the saddle with a quick burst. He rolled over twice and lay still. The pony cantered away and there was only the silence.

They had stopped in a tight group, gazing up towards the circle, but broke almost at once, peeling away to the left and the right to encircle the hill. There didn't seem to be any point in wasting time about opening hostilities, so I tried a snap shot that knocked one out of the saddle immediately.

And then my luck deserted me, or so it seemed, for that wind started to blow again, driving in from the sea, great, heavy rain squalls that dropped a grey curtain over everything.

There was a flash of yellow, a pony coming in from my left, stretched to the limit, the rider low over its neck. I had only time for a short burst and swung as hooves drummed in from directly behind. That one almost made it, riding in at full tilt, sword raised and I emptied the AK into him and jumped out of the way. The pony carried straight on through the circle and out the other side, the rider still upright in the saddle.

I got another clip out of the pouch at my belt and rammed it home as hooves drummed again – so many different directions that I didn't know what to expect next. I compromised by emptying the AK blindly into the mist and rain in several short bursts, taking care of as many points of the compass as I could.

That seemed to cool them off for a while and I feverishly reloaded and slumped down against one of the stones to get my breath.

Helen was watching me, eyes wide, staring.

'They're going to kill you,' she said dully. 'You don't have a chance.'

'As good a way to go as any,' I said. 'Toll for the brave.' I patted the stone I was leaning against. 'This thing's seen it all for the past three or four thousand years. I won't be the first.'

But if I were to go, they would have a hard time of it, I promised myself that. I loaded the M79 with the last grenade and took the smoke grenades out of their pouches, laying them ready in a neat row. At least they might frighten the ponies.

It was then that the first firing started, neatly disposing of my theory about honour and the way of the sword and dying according to the old ritual.

Bullets ricocheted from the stones, whined away into space for perhaps a minute. Then there was silence and in that silence the drum of hooves from several directions at once.

The strategy was plain, but by then, death had become a matter of indifference to me. I jumped to my feet, emptied the AK in a wide arc into the rain on full automatic, shoved in a second clip instantly and repeated the performance in another direction.

I certainly hit something to judge from the disturbance and rammed another clip home and swung as two of them charged out of the greyness, shoulder-to-shoulder from the other side, sword in hand. I gave them the whole magazine, one of them bouncing across the ground, coming to rest across Helen's legs. I shoved him away with my foot, but he was already dead.

The wind changed again, ripping the curtain away, exposing the shambles on the hillside, at least seven or eight bodies sprawled out there, some still alive, voices calling for aid, ponies wandering aimlessly.

They were strung out at the bottom of the hill – at least twenty of them. Some on ponies and some dismounted. At that distance it was not possible to see if St Claire or Chen-Kuen were there, but it was certainly too good a chance to miss.

I raised the M79 to my shoulder, aiming high, remembering it was down hill and fired the last grenade. It landed in the exact centre of the line and I followed it with a smoke grenade for good measure.

It was only then, at the sight of that thick, grey-black cloud rising into the rain like a living thing that it occurred to me that it might still be possible to get out of there. I had two spare clips of ammunition left in the pouch which wasn't going to last me for long, especially if they decided to repeat the earlier performance. I pulled out the bayonet from its sheath at my belt and clipped it in place.

Helen said weakly, 'Still taking on the whole world, Ellis?'

'Something like that. I'm moving out. You just lie low and wait. Whatever happens, you win. Neither side's going to harm you.'

I dropped to one knee and fired off the smoke grenades one after the other in a neat pattern to cover the entire hillside and allowing for the wind.

There was bound to be confusion down there now and I intended to take full advantage of it. I fixed my bayonet on the end of the AK and port ready for action, just like the drill book. I could hear voices, ran past a couple of the wounded or dying, then came across exactly what I was looking for – one of the riderless ponies.

I swung into the saddle and urged it forward, taking my direction from the slope of the hill, trying to move away from the carnage below. So thick was the smoke by now that I almost defeated my own purpose.

I was aware of movement on either side, voices calling, ponies neighing and my own mount was proving difficult to control one-handed for he was obviously terrified in the smoke.

But I see now that it was all a nightmare from the beginning, no meaning to any of it, no sense and this was just another scene from hell.

Perhaps, because of that, it seemed entirely appropriate when Brigadier-General James Maxwell St Claire rode out of the fog to confront me.

By then, I had come to expect such turns and it was St Claire who was the most astonished of the two. I could have killed him then for although he wore a cartridge belt and bayonet at the waist like my own, his MI6 rifle was slung behind his back and I already had him covered with the AK.

He brushed it aside as if it did not exist, a patina of sweat on his face. 'Where's Helen? What have you done with her?'

'Back there on the hill. A scratch on the face, that's all. She'll survive. Is anyone left down there?'

'Enough to see you off, boy. They'll run you into the ground now.' He shook his head, a kind of awe in his voice. 'You are hell on wheels, boy. I should have remembered that.' And then, as if an afterthought, 'Aren't you going to kill me?'

I shook my head. 'Thirty years, Max, that's what they'll give you. I only wish it could be on Devil's Island.'

I got through to him with that all right. Hurt him, I think in some personal way and it is hard to escape the thought that in the end, after all that had happened, my opinion of him was still something he regarded as important.

I put my heels into the pony and galloped away along the hillside, away from the cries of the dying, the confused stamping of the horses.

A moment later, I burst out of the smoke into the freshness of the rain, the green hillside, woods to the left of me, a carpet of tussocky grass stretching down to a scattering of pine trees that dropped into a gully which presumably sloped to a beach below.

I reined-in to take my bearings, there was a single shot and the pony seemed to leap into the air, then started to go down. I managed to roll clear, still clutching the AK, turned and saw seven or eight horsemen on the brow of the hill below the smoke, saw something else in the same moment, coming in low over the sea out of the rain – three Siebe Martin assault helicopters.

Hilary Vaughan and the cavalry arriving at the end of things, but too late for Ellis Jackson. The horsemen fanned out and started to charge on. I emptied most of my magazine at them wildly as I sprawled there on the ground, kicking up earth in great fountains. At least it scattered the ponies for a moment and I scrambled to my feet. If I could reach the wood there might still be hope and I ran for all I was worth, blood in my mouth, not that I stood any kind of chance.

One rider curved in between me and the trees. I fired from the waist on the run and caught him somewhere or other for he swayed in the saddle. I veered sharply to the left, firing again at point-blank range as another cut across my line of vision.

There were still a few rounds left in the magazine and I decided to hang on to them for as the six remaining riders herded me back towards the cliff edge, I saw that only one of them was armed, presumably the man who had shot my pony.

The rest had only the long ivory-handled swords slung beneath the left armpit, each man in wide sleeved yellow robe and wearing a death band round the head.

The man with the rifle tossed it to one side, vaulted from the saddle and drew his sword. He raised it high above his head in true *kendo* style.

I had first handled a rifle and bayonet at the tender age of fourteen in the officer's training corps at school. The Academy, Benning, hand-to-hand fighting in the trenches at Do San – you might say we'd been together a long time.

At any rate, I knew my business. He turned his back and posed – all the showy technique in the world – then swung with one hell of a cry and delivered a basic *do* cut to the right side of the chest. I parried with ease and pointed. He retreated, trapped by his training, the technique hard-learned over the years, turned his back on me and posed again, so I gave him the bayonet below the shoulder blades and slightly to the left, penetrating the heart and killing him instantly. Then I blew him off the end with a quick burst which proved to be the last of my magazine.

There was no time to reload, a moment only in which his companions sat their mounts in stunned silence and then they were out of the saddle, swords unsheathed, gleaming dully in the grey morning.

Five against one. Big odds, even for little Ellis Jackson, although this lot were so crazy I suspected they might come in one at a time. I never found out, for a sudden cry tore the morning in two and St Claire galloped down the hill and reined-in beside the other ponies.

* * *

The monks hesitated, turning towards him as if expecting orders. What happened then was the most surprising thing of all, yet not surprising in the final analysis, for he ran through them, unslinging his rifle and fixing bayonet, taking up his position beside me.

He smiled at me once, that famous St Claire smile, then turned to face them. 'Who dies first?' he called in Chinese.

The last 'banzai'

12

I know now that he was seeking his death. A warrior's end, the best way out, when all was said and done, for a man like him.

But there was no time to consider the implications of his act for with a concerted cry that would have done credit to the Imperial Japanese Guard's last *banzai* in their final battle of the Second World War, the five of them came in like one man.

Two chose me and three, not unnaturally, settled for St Claire. As I parried the first cut, I was aware in a detached sort of way of one of the helicopters dropping down behind the rim of the hill, presumably to the scene of the battle where smoke curled thickly into the air, but that wasn't going to help us here.

The tip of a blade nicked my right arm, I

twisted, gave my opponent the butt under the chin and flung myself to one side as the other's blade sliced at my head.

St Claire had put one man down, was backed up against the ultimate edge of the cliff now, blood on his face, holding off the other two.

I slipped on the wet grass and rolled wildly to avoid the slashing blade that hacked at my head. It missed by a matter of inches, biting deep into the turf and I gave him the bayonet up under the breastbone with both hands.

As I turned to scramble up, one of St Claire's assailants managed to get in close, clutching him by the left arm, smothering the rifle, leaving the way clear for his companion to deliver the death blow.

Strange, but in that moment he was my dearest friend again and my only thought was to aid him. I gave a terrible cry, jumped in and bayoneted the one with the sword in the back.

Not that it did St Claire much good in the end for the other, sensing, I suppose, that all was lost, suddenly pushed with all his strength and they both went over the edge.

* * *

It was a drop of a hundred feet at least to where the sea sprawled in across jagged black rocks in a carpet of white foam, boiling ceaselessly. That anyone could survive such a fall didn't seem possible except for the uncertain chance of dropping into a patch of deep water between the rocks, but as I looked down, St Claire appeared miraculously like some great dark seal.

And yet he was badly injured – had to be for he was unable to help himself and the current took him out across the rocks in a sudden swirl, leaving him sprawled face-down across a mattress of seaweed.

To the right of me, the ground sloped steeply to the start of a reasonably large gully. I skidded along the slope on the wet grass and found the gully to be a wide funnel partially choked with sand and clay, probably a natural outfall for rainwater.

I went down without pause in a shower of earth and sand, still clutching my rifle in one hand. The last twenty or thirty feet or so were virtually perpendicular, but the sand on the beach at that spot was soft and white and broke my fall very effectively.

I could see him clearly now out there on a kind of peninsula of rock which jutted into the sea. As another wave broke over him, I dropped the rifle, ran across the beach and waded through the shallows towards the rocks.

I seemed to hear my name, thought at first it was perhaps St Claire, but this was from another direction. I turned, waist-deep in water. Further along the cliffs, the pine trees flooded down in a great fold, spreading into a gently sloping hillside of grass merging into sand that gave easy access to the beach.

A horseman had paused half-way down – Colonel Chen-Kuen in yellow robes, black quilted *shuba* and death band, scarlet tails fluttering behind. He came down the rest of the bank in a great sliding apron of sand, put spurs to the pony and was across the beach and into the shallows like a thunderbolt, the sword streaking from its scabbard.

And I had nothing, but empty hands and waited there for him, waited for the steel to descend. But in the last moment, he was victim of his own peculiar notions of honour, realised my weaponless state, reined in his mount and sheathed the sword.

He sat there looking at me gravely, holding the pony in tightly as it moved nervously from side to side, an unforgettable picture in those mediaeval robes, vivid against the grey sky.

'I always underestimated you, Ellis,' he said and then leapt at me from the saddle, arms outstretched.

I went down under his weight, but at the same moment a wave swept in and turned the world upside down. When I surfaced again he was three or four yards away.

He ploughed towards me, assuming a martial stance. It was all to be according to the book, I realised this now. A solemn ritual between equal adversaries. Almost a religious rite.

He gave the usual courage shout, then threw a reverse punch which takes the uninitiated unawares as it is delivered with the hand on the same side as the rear foot.

I evaded it with a right block, pivoted and delivered a reverse elbow strike that caught him full in the mouth, breaking teeth. Another wave washed us apart and as the swell subsided, he came in with a rush, delivering one blow after another at my head with the edge of his hands. I countered with the *juji-uke*, the X-block and got another elbow strike into his face.

A second wave swept in, much larger this time, driving me back towards the rocks in a welter of dirty brown foam. He was on his feet before I was that time, catching me in the left ribs with with a reverse punch, screwing it in with all his force, all his energy focussed on that one place.

I could feel at least two ribs go and dropped to one side and delivered a roundhouse kick to his groin, awkwardly because of the water. He went down and I gave him an old-fashioned punch in the stomach at close quarters and moved in close as he keeled over. It was a mistake for he erupted from the water with incredible speed and energy, the edge of his hand striking with all the cutting force of that sword of his.

He broke my left arm with that single, devastating blow, would have had me cold a second later if another great wave had not smashed in across us. I went deep in a maelstrom of green water and surfaced to find him floundering a good fifteen yards away. It was all I needed and I plunged towards the shore.

As I staggered up on to the beach, I glanced over my shoulder and saw him wading towards his pony. After that, I put down my head and ran like hell towards that narrow funnel in the cliff where I had descended.

The hooves were already drumming as I dropped to one knee beside the AK. I didn't bother looking over my shoulder, simply concentrated on getting the final clip out of the ammunition belt at my waist and into the rifle and I had only one usable hand, remember.

He cried my name out loud once, perhaps recognising his executioner and greeting me, or perhaps an appeal for me to play the game his way and with honour, man-to-man to the end.

I turned, dropped to one knee, poked the AK out in front of me one-handed and shot him in the head. It was only then, as he tumbled backwards out of the saddle, that I realised that he hadn't even bothered to draw his sword.

* * *

A helicopter soared in over the cliffs, moving out to sea, turned and came closer, seeking a safe place to land, a difficult thing to do on that narrow beach with the down-draughts always to be found in such an area.

I had more important things on my mind and ran back across the sand, one arm dangling uselessly and ploughed through the shallows to the rocks.

By some miracle he was still in sight, a little further out now on a ledge of rock jutting over deep water to one side. By rights he should already have been dead, but presumably a chance wave had left him there. It would only take one more to finish him, to wipe him from the face of memory forever.

It was necessary to climb down to get to that particular point and the boulders were slippery and treacherous, covered with seaweed and green slime that would have made the going hard in normal circumstances, but with my broken arm, almost impossible.

I made it – had to and nothing above this earth or beneath it could have stopped me. Water boiled in again, sending me back against a boulder, spraying knee-deep and somewhere my name was called. When I turned, there were men up there on the rocks by the shore in camouflage jump jackets and red berets.

I floundered on, knee-deep, convinced that he must have gone, fell forward on the edge at last and looked over to the ledge below.

He was still there, eyes tight shut as if in pain and when he opened them and saw me, there was immediate recognition. He raised his left arm, I reached out my right, found his hand and held on tight.

'Now then you old bastard.'

'Did you sort them out, boy? Did you dust them up good?'

'Right down the line.'

'I always did say you had qualities. I'm not going to say I'm sorry. No point. You should have learned the truth of life by now.'

'Who's asking you?'

A wave washed in across us. Those paratroopers were very close now. He said, 'Okay, Ellis, let go.'

'Like hell I will.'

'Thirty years, boy, and a cripple at that. Is

that what you want? Will that mean it never happened?'

He smiled, that famous St Claire smile and something like bile rose in my throat to choke me, I sobbed out loud, at the end of something at last, holding him tight till the next wave came, then letting it take him with it as it receded.

I saw him once more, the face dark against the white foam out there and then he was gone.

It was perhaps a minute later, not more, that a largish individual in a camouflaged uniform, ploughed through the foam and got a grip on me. I turned, clutching at his leg with my one good hand and looked up at Hilary Vaughan.

He pulled me up and we stood there, water ebbing about our knees and he waved his men back. I said, 'I let him go.'

He nodded. 'Best thing under the circumstances.'

'For whom?'

But he had no answer to that one. Simply took me by the arm with surprising strength and helped me up to where his men waited.

* * *

The helicopter was not too far away, but I sat down on a rock and Vaughan pushed a cigarette into my mouth. 'You cut it rather fine,' I told him.

'I would have thought the boot was on the other foot, old lad,' he said gravely.

'You got what you wanted, didn't you? Are your men having any trouble with the rest of them?'

'I'm using the Guards Parachute Company,' he said. 'Those lads just don't have trouble – not with anybody.'

In the middle distance a familiar figure was running towards us from the helicopter – Helen St Claire, a field dressing taped to her face.

Vaughan glanced over his shoulder and said, 'We picked her up on top – quite hysterical. This might not be pleasant, I warn you.'

She stopped three or four yards away, staring at me uncertainly. 'Max?' she demanded in a strangely querulous way. 'What have you done with Max?'

'Max is dead, Helen,' I said tonelessly.

She might have been carved from stone, so

still was she as she stood there and then she moved very close to me, staring into my face.

'You killed him, didn't you? You killed my brother, you white bastard. You killed my brother.'

She struck me across the face again and again, sobbing hysterically until Vaughan dragged her off. He held her for a moment until she seemed quieter, then released her. She turned and ran back along the shore towards the helicopter.

I don't suppose I was capable of rational thought then. I said to him, 'You lied to me, didn't you? You knew all about St Claire from the beginning.'

He nodded. 'The way it had to be, Ellis.'

Like St Claire, he saw no reason to say he was sorry. I watched Helen go, head down, following the shoreline and he said quietly, 'You've lost her, Ellis. You realise that?'

'I never had her,' I turned to look out to sea. 'I never really had anything worth the having.'

'Oh, I don't know. You've done well, Ellis. Exceptionally well. We could use you – in the future, I mean, when you've got over all this.'

I found that so funny, I could have laughed

out loud. Instead, I simply shook my head. 'I don't think so.'

'I wouldn't be too sure. Give yourself time. After all, what will you do now? It would be some kind of solution. A damned sight better than going back to that cottage in the marshes.'

He could have been right, very probably was, but not then – not by any stretch of the imagination. I stood up and stared out at the grey waters, looking for St Claire, listening for his voice, the slightest indication that he had ever existed, and failed. Then I turned and infinitely slowly, because I was suddenly very tired, walked away along the shore.

Bad Company

Jack Higgins

Wartime secrets threaten to topple a President – in the heart-stopping new adventure from the incomparable Jack Higgins.

In the waning days of World War II, Hitler entrusted his diary to a young aide, Baron Max von Berger. Over the years, von Berger has used his inheritance to become one of the richest men in the world, developing a secret alliance with the Rashid family – long-time foes of Major Ferguson of British Intelligence, his undercover enforcer Sean Dillon and their American colleague Blake Johnson. Now the ultimate confrontation is drawing near. The diary and its explosive revelations of a secret wartime meeting between emissaries of Hitler and Roosevelt will destroy the US President Jake Cazalet . . . unless Dillon can find it first.

'A Master craftsmen at the peak of his powers . . . first-rate tales of intrigue, suspense and full-on action.'

Sunday Express

0-00-712718-9

A Fine Night for Dying

Jack Higgins

The death of a gangster draws super-spy Paul Chavasse into a breathtaking adventure on the high seas – an unforgettable tale from one of the true masters of modern thriller writing.

Caught in the nets of a local fishing boat, the body of gangland boss Harvey Preston is dragged from the English Channel, wrapped from head to toe in heavy chain. British intelligence suspects a connection with a cross-channel smuggling ring. But as undercover agent Paul Chavasse embarks on what will be one of the most dangerous cases in his extraordinary career, he soon discovers that this is no small-time operation – and the ruthless men behind it will stop at nothing to protect their precious cargo.

'Open a Jack Higgins novel and you'll encounter a master craftsman at the peak of his powers . . . first-rate tales of intrigue, suspense and full-on action.' *Sunday Express*

'The master craftsman of good, clean adventure.'
Daily Mail

0 00 712720 0